THE COMPETITION

Also by **Maddie Ziegler**

The Maddie Diaries
The Audition
The Callback

MADDIE ZIEGLER

THE COMPETITION

with Julia DeVillers

ALADDIN
New York   London   Toronto   Sydney   New Delhi

ALADDIN

An imprint of Simon & Schuster Children's Publishing Division

1230 Avenue of the Americas, New York, New York 10020

First Aladdin paperback edition October 2020

Text © 2019 by M, M & M, Inc.

Cover illustrations © 2019 by Magdalina Dianova

Also available in an Aladdin hardcover edition.

All rights reserved, including the right of reproduction in whole or in part in any form.

ALADDIN and related logo are registered trademarks of Simon & Schuster, Inc.

For information about special discounts for bulk purchases, please contact Simon & Schuster Special Sales at 1-866-506-1949 or business@simonandschuster.com.

The Simon & Schuster Speakers Bureau can bring authors to your live event. For more information or to book an event contact the Simon & Schuster Speakers Bureau at 1-866-248-3049 or visit our website at www.simonspeakers.com.

Book design by Laura DiSiena

The text of this book was set in Miller Text.

Manufactured in the United States of America 0920 OFF

2 4 6 8 10 9 7 5 3 1

The Library of Congress has cataloged the hardcover edition as follows:

Names: Ziegler, Maddie, author.

Title: The competition / by Maddie Ziegler ; with Julia DeVillers.

Description: First Aladdin hardcover edition. | New York : Aladdin, 2019. |

Series: Maddie Ziegler ; 3 | Summary: When Harper and her fellow Dance Starz go to New York City for nationals, they not only face their arch-rivals, the Bells, but Harper will also compete against her old dance team. |

Identifiers: LCCN 2019016550 (print) | LCCN 2019019239 (eBook) |

ISBN 9781481486446 (eBook) | ISBN 9781481486422 (hc)

Subjects: | CYAC: Dance—Fiction. | Competition (Psychology)—Fiction. | Friendship—Fiction. | Family life—Florida—Fiction. | Florida—Fiction. | New York (N.Y.)—Fiction. | BISAC: JUVENILE FICTION / Performing Arts / Dance. | JUVENILE FICTION / Social Issues / Friendship. | JUVENILE FICTION / Social Issues / New Experience.

Classification: LCC PZ7.1.Z54 (eBook) | LCC PZ7.1.Z54 Com 2019 (print) | DDC [Fic]—dc23

LC record available at https://lccn.loc.gov/2019016550

ISBN 9781481486439 (pbk)

"Welcome to . . . regionals!" the announcer's voice rings throughout the packed convention center.

This is it. Regionals. And all eyes are on us. This is the moment! We are here! My costume is super cute. It's black and pink, with some flowy ribbons dangling off my shoulders. That sounds weird, but it works. I have a little hat on my head, tilted just right and securely fastened by approximately a thousand bobby pins.

At least I hope it's securely fastened. That would be bad if my hat fell off, wouldn't it? Ha! Okay, that's actually not funny. If my hat falls off, then I might trip over it. Or one of my dance squad might trip over it, and slide all the way across the stage—not just across the stage! Off the stage! Onto the judge's table, knocking everything over and destroying the entire regionals!

My best friend and teammate, Lily, grabbed my hand and squeezed it hard, snapping me out of my imaginary list of things that could go wrong.

"Harper!" Lily whispered to me. "I think my hat is loose!"

"I was JUST thinking mine was," I whispered back.

"That's why we're best friends," Lily said. "You understand me."

Lily and I had become best friends ever since I'd moved to Florida. Lily, who had been new to the team too, was the first person I met, right before we'd auditioned for DanceStarz. I remember when I walked in, I was worried I'd never find my place on the team. The rest of the team, aka the Bunheads—Megan, Riley, and Trina—hadn't exactly been welcoming at first, to either of us. So Lily and I had bonded over that, and then become true friends, totally on the same page. Like for example, worrying about our hats falling off.

"Were you also thinking you'd trip on it, slide across the stage, and fall on the judges and the competition would come to a screeching halt and the judges would toss you out the door of the building?" I whispered.

"Um, no?" Lily said. "I take it back. I guess I don't understand you."

We both cracked up a little.

"Are you two laughing? No laughing!" Megan hissed at us. "This is serious business. Regionals."

When I'd first met Megan, I'd been intimidated by her. We'd had our ups and downs, but now we had mutual respect for each other's talent and hard work. We even had fun together. Most of the time.

"First this, and then our duet," Megan said, looking hard at me. "Serious business."

Okay, this was not one of those fun moments. Megan also was very competitive and intense—and my duet partner. Lily and I smiled at each other. It had taken a little while, but we had learned not to let Megan get to us before a competition.

"You're on deck, DanceStarz!" A woman with a clipboard came backstage.

Eek! This was it!

We all gathered around in a tight circle to do the ritual we'd made up as a squad.

"Dance!" Trina led the cheer.

Lily, Megan, Trina, Riley, and I all did a little dance move.

"Starz!" Trina continued.

We fluttered our fingers like sparkling stars. Then we leaned into a huddle and said:

"Squad!"

DanceStarz Squad was ready to take the stage! *HERE WE GO!*

"Make some noise for . . . DanceStarz!" the announcer's voice boomed throughout the packed convention center.

On that cue, we flashed out best smiles and stepped onstage in formation, our arms swinging in perfect sync. We sashayed to our positions, and we struck a pose and waited under the hot lights for the music. I had one hand on my hip and one in the air, steady. I took a moment to take it all in—the excited charge in the air, the supportive cheers. Yes. This was it. We'd worked so hard to get to this point. We'd edged out the fiercest including the team from competitive Energii, our biggest rivals. All that would be left for us to do is perform our hearts out. A solid show here would advance us to nationals, which—

Which I couldn't think about right now. I had to focus and go into my zone. This is when all of my training, my muscle memory, all of those hard rehearsals pay off. My brain shuts down, and my body takes over.

The music began. And I danced. We used to watch ourselves in the dance studio mirrors, but now the crowd is our only reflection. From the roar of the crowd, we were delivering the goods. Our leg extensions must have been showing off the flowy chiffon trailing from the backs of our shoulders. The pretty fabric swirls looked like a ribbon dance. Finally, that last beat dropped. We bowed and trotted offstage to extended applause.

Vanessa was the first to greet us offstage. "Beautiful," she said, beaming proudly. She's our dance team teacher and our choreographer AND owner of the DanceStarz Studio. We all grabbed one another in a big hug and jumped around to celebrate.

We got two seconds of celebration before Vanessa cleared her throat.

"Duets, get ready."

Annnnd our killer performance was already a thing of the past. Lily and I went to give each other extra hugs.

"You got this," she whispered.

"Same!" I told her. It's a huge day for Lily. She got picked to be the solo dancer, and will be going last.

"Harper!" Megan hissed at me. "Let's go!"

I rushed to the shared backstage changing area to change costumes, into the sparkly deep purple leotard we picked out together. The farther we walked away from the rest of the squad, the more tense it felt to be alone with Megan.

"Remember," she said. "Vanessa changed the high kick in the end to a split jump."

"Yeah," I agreed. "And don't forget the arabesque to the new twirl move."

"I know that. Don't worry about whether *I* have all our moves down," she said dismissively. "Concentrate on yourself."

"You started this," I said, annoyed. "Duets are all about

making sure we're both on the same page. We have to help each other shine."

Megan snorted. I knew what was bothering her—again. She was still bitter that she didn't get the first-ever solo. We all had wanted that solo—but I was still super happy for Lily.

"It's Lily, not us, in the solo today," I reminded her.

"That doesn't mean I can't prove that I'm solo material," Megan muttered.

So that was her plan. She wanted to stand out in the duet in the hopes she'd get the next solo. That's a risky move, because nowhere in the word "duet" are the letters *s-o-l-o*. And, PS, the next solo was a big one, because it was nationals! Yes, if we placed high enough today, then we got to go to nationals and nationals this year . . . in NEW YORK CITY!

Then again, Megan has a point. The only person I should focus on was myself at the moment. I wanted to finish strong at regionals. I didn't want to let down the Squad! I didn't want let down DanceStarz, the studio I represent! And I didn't want to let myself down! I worked too hard for this.

We headed down the hall to the changing rooms. Regionals dressing rooms were an upgrade from the local competition. DanceStarz had our own corner, and Megan's and my mom were waiting for us.

"Great job, sweetheart!" My mom gave me a big hug. "Did you have fun?"

"Fun?" Megan's mother turned around. "This is not time for chitchat. They need to get ready for their big duet."

Mom raised an eyebrow at me.

"Don't engage," I whispered.

"Don't let her add to your stress." Mom smiled at me. Then she frowned. "Where are the girls' costumes?"

"Oh, I had my assistant do a last-minute steaming," Megan's mother said. "No wrinkles, only perfection. She's bringing them in now."

We went and sat down in front of the tables set up with mirrors. Megan and I didn't say anything while our moms helped us with our hair—except for the occasional "ouch" when the bobby pins got yanked out of our hat heads. My mom cleaned up all the pins and took the hat. We both know, though, that I'm better at doing my own hair than she is, so she let me finish. My hair was a little ratty from the bobby pins, so I brushed it out and pulled it up into a high ponytail.

"Mom?" I called her over and swung my pony back and forth.

"Wispie-free!" she said. "Nice and smooth."

"Where are our leotards? She is taking forever." Megan was

complaining. Megan's mom's assistant (I still couldn't believe she had an assistant) walked in with our leotards on hangers. "Give me mine!"

Megan grabbed hers, and then the assistant handed me mine. It was really pretty—a burgundy long-sleeved leotard we wore with a matching vest that had crystals embellished on it. It also was warm from being steamed.

"Break your legs!" my mom called out and left with Megan's mom to head to their seats in the audience.

I pulled on my costume—and noticed something weird. The leotard sleeves seemed a little long. *Huh.* Maybe steaming wrinkles out lengthened them. Megan came over wearing an identical outfit and ponytail.

"You look great," I told her. She was pulling at her sleeve. "Hey, is your sleeve bugging you, too? Mine feels stretched out."

"No," Megan said, pulling at her other sleeve.

"Why are you pulling at it?" I asked her.

"I think my arms grew. Yes! My arms may have lengthened because I've been doing all of my stretches in preparation for today. It will make my lines look amazing."

"Wait, if your sleeves are weird too, then—"

"Really? You're complaining right before our duet? Are you

trying to bring me down with your negative energy?" Megan asked me.

"What? No, I just thought it's weird that—"

Vanessa walked in the door. She looked at us both and immediately picked up the tension.

"Let's see that partnership shine out there," she said. "Any missteps will be more obvious, so remember you're in this together, girls."

"Yes, Vanessa." We both nodded, our ponytails bobbing.

Megan pretty much should have said *No, Vanessa*. When we took the stage, the music started—and Megan went into solo mode.

Step, high kick, and . . . What in the world was going on?! Megan took an extra step forward, hogging the spotlight. I tried to give her a side eye, but she gave me a toothy smile back. Her face was wide-eyed and expressive, working the audience. There was hardly any connection between us. The only connection I was feeling was between her and the audience. I guessed I had to just focus on myself. I twirled (yes, twice), did my turn series, and kicked. Then we got ready for our signature partner trick. This one relied on us being perfectly in sync.

Megan did a leap toward me, looking like she was going to

crash into me. I knew the audience would be at full attention, and so did Megan. She gave them a dramatic, overly surprised face. Then she slid forward on the ground so that she was right underneath my leg. Just as my leg would have hit her, she melted down into a hinge.

I twirled my leg horizontally over her, and then popped up. Then I twirled back over her, and she ducked down over and over. I finished with a turn holding my leg high and straight, with Megan underneath me, and held it for a few seconds. We did it perfectly! Yes! Whew! Then I brought my leg down and spun. Megan stepped in front of me, which by then I was getting used to. But that's when it happened.

Megan did a big swoop with her arm. She overdid her arm reach and tore her long-sleeved leotard, just under her arm. The seam split. She froze.

I couldn't help it: My first thought was *Serves you right*. My second thought was what Vanessa said, though—we are partners, and we're supposed to support each other. My third thought was that if Megan looks bad, I look bad.

My fourth thought was: *How do we cover it up?* I think that was Megan's only thought, from her panicky look.

When we spun with our backs to the audience, I mouthed to her: *I got you.*

I adjusted our dance and took action, positioning myself to cover her holey-ness with my body. Megan regrouped to let me block her. The result was a synchronized mirror image of poses that unfolded pretty well.

We ran offstage. Megan was clutching her arm. Riley and Trina were waiting in the hall, hair in buns, dressed in pink-and-butter-yellow dresses for their duet.

"Megan, you were awesome," Riley said.

"I can't believe this happened!" Megan was visibly upset. She ripped off the vest and threw it on the floor. "I'm suing the costume place."

"Oh, no!" Trina said. "Because they got your name wrong?"

"Huh?" We all looked at her, confused.

Trina picked up the vest off the floor and showed it to us. The label pinned into it said HARPER.

"Wait," I said. I pulled my vest off. Sure enough, it said MEGAN. No wonder my sleeves didn't fit—Megan had longer arms than I did.

"Harper wore my outfit, and my sleeve ripped!" Megan wailed. "It screwed up everything."

"WHAT?" I protested. "You're the one who grabbed it after your mother's assistant—"

"Oh. Whatever. That doesn't matter," Megan said. "What matters is my leo ripped onstage at regionals."

I saw Vanessa waving pointedly at us.

"Actually, I think what matters is Riley and Trina's duet onstage," I said, tilting my head toward Vanessa.

"Where are your priorities? I am not very happy right now," Megan snarled.

"I won't be happy either if our next duet doesn't take the stage on time," Vanessa said from behind us. Megan's face turned white.

"I meant, Riley! Trina! Go, team, go!" Megan recovered quickly.

Megan and I were done, so we went into the audience. All the parents were in seats. My little sister, Hailey, was waving at me to sit next to her. I went up the aisle and started to slide into the seat.

"Not you, Harper," she said. "I was saving the seat for Megan!"

Blugh. Megan turned around and smirked at me. Hailey loved Megan. Megan was actually really good with younger kids. On the bright side, I didn't have to sit next to my sister, who wiggled a lot.

I slid into a seat behind my mom. We all watched Riley and Trina do their jazz solo, cheering them on. They did great!

Trina was on point as always with her precision and her footwork, and Riley really worked the crowd.

"Go Riley! Go Trina!" I called out.

When the next duet came out, I heard Megan give an audible sigh.

"Let's give it up for a duet from the studio Energii!" the announcer called out. The two girls who came out were the Bells. They used to be on the DanceStarz competition team until they went to a new studio. They also had been Megan's teammates and so-called best friends. They hadn't been particularly nice to any of us since I'd moved here. They took the stage and did a modern routine that was truly impressive. When the crowd went wild for them, I clapped loudly, but Megan was subdued watching them dance. I knew it must hurt when your friends moved on.

It made me think about my friends from my old dance team in Connecticut. We still talked and liked each other's stuff on social, but I wondered what it would be like if I saw them in person. Would they have moved on? Would it hurt? Would I find out soon?

If we won regionals, I actually might have a chance to see them in person. Ack! One of a million reasons I really wanted to win today. My nerves didn't have a chance to go away, because right after the Bells danced—and, okay, got a lot of lot of applause—it was time for solos.

Including DanceStarz's first solo, starring Lily! She was first up, and as she took the stage, I let out a loud cheer. I hoped she could hear me! "Go Lily, go Lily!" I yelled.

I looked at Lily's parents down the row, looking nervous. I was nervous for her too. I heard the announcer introduce her.

"This is Lily from DanceStarz, performing a jazz gymnastics routine, 'Flip to It'!"

I shouldn't have been nervous. Lily didn't disappoint. Lily had been putting in extra hours, including privates with Vanessa, and it showed. Lily had taken gymnastics all her life, and her aerials and backflips were on point. We all cheered like crazy for her. The rest of the crowd did too, and I watched her parents beaming with pride.

There were some awesome solos. After they were over, we all ran to our dressing room. I practically jumped into Lily's arms.

"Did you see me?" Lily asked me, in a state of disbelief.

"You looked amazing out there!" I squeezed her tight. "Did you hear the love you got from the crowd?"

"The crowd was into it!" Riley chimed in.

"It was like watching the Olympics! You were like flip! Handspring! Boop! Upside down back walkover, woot!" Trina bubbled, and Lily smiled.

And then . . . crickets. We all look at Megan.

"Um, that back walkover *was* woot," she said sincerely.

Lily's smile was contagious. Just like me, she was the new-comer to DanceStarz Academy, and had to prove herself to Vanessa and the Squad.

"You proved us wrong," Megan said.

"You mean proved us right?" I said.

"No, we didn't think she could do it," Megan said. "Thus, she proved us wrong."

"Uh, thanks?" Lily said. "I think?"

Vanessa came in and told Lily SHE WAS PROUD OF HER! Yes! I wanted this moment to last forever for her. I was super proud of her too.

"Hit the stage, my select team," Vanessa said. "Time for results. This is it, girls."

Eep. Trophy time! (Or no-trophy time!) A backstage wrangler dressed in all black and wearing a headset ushered us to a roped-off contestants' bullpen in front of the stage. We sat in a tight huddle and listened anxiously. The lights shone in our faces, and we could kind of see the audience waiting in suspense as the announcer went on and on about how the judges tally the points—adding or subtracting points for choreography, execution, stage presence, and difficulty. And then, finally, it was time.

First up, the solos. Lily got third! Lily got to jump onstage and get a small trophy and stand with the top three!

"Top three!" I practically shrieked at her when she sat down.

"It's not first place, sorry," Lily said, worried.

"Yeah." Riley rolled her eyes, looking at Megan for confirmation.

"Nobody was expecting first place," Megan said. We all looked at her. "What? I'm trying to say third place is good for regionals. It's top three, trophy, and good to keep us all in the running for nationals."

Wow! I had to agree with Megan there. Lily smiled.

"Let's move on to the duets!" the announcer called out. Suddenly, a hand gripped mine. Megan's. I gripped it back. They announced the fourth-place duet. Then, third place was . . . Riley and Trina!

"Third placers!" Lily held her fist up to bump when they sat down with their trophies. Trina bumped happily; Riley, not so much. I barely noticed because Megan was squeezing my hand so hard.

"First place, first place," she whispered. I could see she was side-eyeing the Bells, who were ignoring her a little too obviously.

"Second-place duet is . . . DanceStarz Academy!"

We got second. A loud squeal came up from the Bells, who were stomping the floor.

"You get the trophy," Megan whispered. I figured she'd want the glory, but I guess it was hard to get second place in front of the Bells. But second place was great! Top three! Especially with that ripped leotard. I was happy to go up and accept the trophy. I could hear my parents and sister cheering for me. Yay us!

Then it was time for the grand finale, the big one, the group dance, the opportunity to go to nationals. . . . It was all coming down to this moment.

"Our final category is Group Dance! In third place, Energii!"

What? Third? We all looked at each other as we clapped. Third? They're a go-hard squad who consider second place a crushing defeat. Sure enough, they headed to the stage with sour faces. Isabella and Bella avoided eye contact with the bullpen contestants as they went up to get their trophy.

"Do you think we actually beat them? Do you think we got second?" Lily whispered to me.

"In second place, the Groove Thangz!" The crowd cheers, and the team in dazzling gold jumpsuits who did a hip-hop routine happily accept their trophy.

That threw everything upside down. Number two is our usual spot. Did we not rank at all? Or . . . or . . . We all held our breaths. *Say DanceStarz, say DanceStarz . . .*

"And our number one group dance is . . . DanceStarz!"

Oh. My. Gosh. We did it! We did it!

WE WON!!

We screamed and jumped up and down all the way up to the stage. Megan took the trophy first, and then held it out so we could hoist it in the air together. I saw my mom, dad, and little sister, Hailey, in the crowd waving their homemade DANCESTARZ sign like crazy!

"THAT'S MY SISTER!" Haley screamed, and I spotted her doing a high-five thing with Riley's sister, Quinn. Maybe someday they'd be up on the stage too. Lily, Riley, Trina, Megan, and I gave each other a genuine group hug. We'd proven something to ourselves. And we'd proven we were ready to compete on a national stage. NATIONALS.

New York City, HERE WE COME!

ree fro-yo for the number one dance team of all time!"
said Lily's father, beaming from behind the counter.

"Well, that's a bit much." Lily smiled at him.

"It won't be!" Megan said. "After we go to New York City and win nationals!"

We all held up our yogurts and smoothies and did a "cheers."

The four of us took a seat at the round table by the window. I dug into my cheesecake yogurt topped with blackberries and whipped cream. I looked across the palm-tree-lined plaza at the front façade of DanceStarz Academy. They'd already placed a banner out front: HOME OF THE DANCESTARZ SQUAD— REGIONAL CHAMPS. I smiled at that—and at the sight of the tiniest dancers milling into the studio for a peewee dance class. That was how young I was when I got started back home in Connecticut. I loved it from the start.

"This is the best celebration ever," Trina said. "Also the best yogurt."

"What even is on that?" Megan looked at Trina's overflowing bowl.

"Candy corn, cinnamon cereal, brownie bites, kiwi, gummy fish, pretzels, marshmallows," she replied. "Oh my gosh, I forgot to put yogurt in it."

We all laughed as Trina stood up to go over to the yogurt handles in the wall.

"I cannot believe we are going to New York City," Riley said. "I mean, I am going to live there someday. Right, Megan? We're going to be roommates! I'm going to be a big fashion designer! Megan is going to be a famous dancer and a huge star! Everything is better and bigger in NYC!"

"Like the rats," added Megan.

Lily made a face.

"I'm just saying," said Megan. "Let's be real. It's a pretty tough city. We'll see if you can handle it."

Megan was still the clear queen bee of the Bunheads, the clique she, Trina, and Riley formed way before Lily and I got here.

"I can handle it," Riley whined. "But are you for serious? Rats?"

"Why don't we talk to someone who's actually been there?" said Lily, looking at me. "Harper practically lived there."

"Connecticut is not New York City," Megan pointed out.

"Just a short train ride away," I said, remembering those special trips into the city to see a show or the dazzling holiday lights. This would be my first time going back home. "You're going to love being in New York. There's so much to see."

"Like celebrities!" said Riley, swooning. "I'd give anything to bump into Trey Thompson."

Lily clapped her hands like a baby seal. "He's so dreamy. I love him in *NYC High*!"

"I just want to check out the street fashion," said Megan. "If we go up there and everyone is walking around in schlumpy clothes, I'll be disappointed."

"Great pizza, perfect bagels, yummy cupcakes—trust me, there's something there for everyone," I said.

"My favorite cupcake is that one with the green icing," Trina cooed, sitting back down.

"We're talking about New York ones," Megan said.

"Yeah, my favorite cupcake place is that one in the West Village," Trina said.

"Wait, you've been to New York?" Megan asked her.

"Yeah, I have," Trina said. "You know that I visit my aunt in Midtown for Thanksgiving."

"Well, that's cool," I said. "Trina and I can be the New York experts and show you all around."

"Oh, I always get lost," Trina said. "Harper, *you* can show us all around."

"I practically know New York," Megan grumbled. "Like, I know not to walk too slow and look up at buildings or you look like a tourist. I'm obsessed and totally going to live there someday."

"With me!" Riley added cheerfully.

"I'm so excited!" Lily said. "We're all going to New York together!"

Everyone smiled as they ate their fro-yo and drank their smoothies. I knew we had to keep this team dynamic going. If there was one thing I'd learned, it was that strengthening our team bond was just as important as getting our routines down. We did amazing things when we put team first, and we'd need to be extra tight when we were up against intense competition in New York City.

Even though at some point, we'd have to compete with one another in the solo category. We were all going to be working on getting solos down for the competition too.

"You know who else we'd have to compete against in solos?" I pointed out.

"Yeah, I can't believe Isabella will be there," Riley complained. "How did she get an invite? How did she get enough points?"

"Isabella always gets what she wants." Megan sighed. "I just hope it's not first place at nationals."

4

*A*n overflowing bowl of popcorn in hand, I headed to the living room, where my family was already set up for game night. My malti-poo, Mo, jumped around my feet, hoping for some dropped kernels.

"There she is!" My dad clapped when I joined them. Hailey was sitting on the floor, and my parents were seated around the low coffee table. A board game was set out, along with game pieces, dice, and cards.

"What's with the applause?" I asked him, smiling. "Should I bow or . . ."

"We're just so happy the popcorn is ready!" said Hailey, jumping up taking the bowl from me.

"Actually, we are clapping for Harper and her big win. In honor of your upcoming trip, we thought we'd play a game from my childhood," said Mom.

"Ugggghhh. Mom made Dad dig in the attic again." Hailey spoke and crunched at the same time.

"It's the *Wizard of Oz* game, based on the novel and movie!" said Mom, giving the surprise away before I could look for myself. Mom was not one for suspense.

"Get it?" said Dad, driving the point home. "The main character, Dorothy, is on a quest to get back home. And you'll be heading back to the northeast—your home."

"Remember Connecticut? My room, which was peach and looked out onto that big, leafy tree with Timothy the squirrel? The gray one. I wonder if you'll get to visit Connecticut while you're there," said Hailey dreamily.

"She'll probably be so busy rehearsing and keeping to a tight schedule," answered Mom.

"I don't know." I reach over to Hailey and grab a handful of popcorn. "I hear there's a lot of wait time, because we are staying in town for longer. The competition is only three days."

"Oh, goody," Hailey said. "Say hi to Timothy for me, okay?"

"Any of your old friends competing?" Dad asked.

"I don't know yet," I said.

"Aw, you and Eliza used to be joined at the hip at your old dance studio." Mom smiled at the memory. "I still have so many old pictures of you two in my phone. You didn't tell her?"

"It's just I don't know if they made nationals," I said. "And I don't want to rub it in or brag or anything."

"You could start by saying you're coming to New York," Mom suggested.

"That's actually a good point," I said, pulling out my phone.

"Not now, because it's game time!" Dad said.

I learned that the object of the game was pretty straight-forward. It was a super-cute game for kids way younger than me, but my parents were so happy. Okay, it was kind of fun when the flying monkey game pieces chased us around the board.

After Hailey won, and after I endured her "In your face!" rants, I headed up to my room. I pulled up Eliza's name on my phone.

Guess who's coming to NYC?

It only took three seconds before she texted back with smiley-face emojis.

WHEN?

I hesitated and then just went for it. I texted that I was

coming for nationals. And then the answer that came back made me smile bigger.

Congrats on making it to nationals! We'll be competing too!!!! Well—not our old team. I have news! I made the ELITE TEAM! I'm the youngest on it!!!

We texted back and forth. We were both so excited! I told her I didn't know if I could come to Connecticut, but now we'd be able to hang out in the city together, like we used to!

I smiled. Eliza and I hadn't kept up with texting as much as we did last summer. Things got busy with DanceStarz, and then I had to adjust to going to a new school. But Mom was right. We'd shared so many fun times together. Plus, we made a dope dancing duo. It felt good that she was just as excited to see me as I was to see her.

What are you dancing? I asked her.

Small group, duet, and solo! she texted back. Hbu?

Just small group, I told her. It's my studio's first nationals, so we're only in one category.

Cool! Eliza texted back. But sorry, no offense, we are going to CRUSH you at nationals ;)

Eliza had said what we were both thinking. Well, I'd been thinking *we* would crush *them* at nationals. But still. I plopped down on my bed and stared at the Dance City trophies around my room. My closet door was open, and the rows of bright, sparkly dance competition gear caught my eye. It was a little weird because not so long ago I would have been on that team. Now we would be competing against each other.

I miss uuuu! she texted, and I sent her a happy GIF of our favorite dancer on TV.

I headed to bed even more excited about our trip, but also a little weirded out. My old studio friends and my new studio friends, my old life and new life—all in one place. How mind-blowing was that?

"I wish I could go to New York City," said Zora as she ate the lasagna from her hot lunch. "How fun would that be if the whole cast of *The Little Mermaid* went? We could go to a Broadway show! Then we'd all be discovered and be on Broadway!"

"Not me—crowds make me anxious," said Flounder. Flounder wasn't his real name, of course. His real name was Taj, and he'd played Flounder in the school musical I did recently. And his name had stuck. "I'll stay here."

"I went to New York once," Drew said. Then he smiled at me. Drew had played Prince Eric in the show, and I'd helped him learn his dances. "We went to that Thanksgiving parade.

I remember I was so excited to see SpongeBob, and my mom said I was yelling for his autograph."

We all cracked up.

"I wish you guys could be in the spring musical," Zora said sadly.

"I do, too," I said. But dance was taking up more and more of my time. It had been challenging juggling both before, but now with nationals coming up there was no way. "You know I'll be there to cheer you on."

"It overlaps with baseball practice," Drew said. "We're hoping to get to the tournament. Regionals, not nationals like some special people."

He looked at me and smiled. I smiled back.

"I do want to try out for the fall show," I said. "Dance is sort of calmer in the fall."

"Yay!" Zora said dramatically. "Meantime, soak up some Broadway vibes for me. Yell at all of the theaters: 'Zora is coming for you!'"

We all laughed.

"Trina is going to have to miss our battle-of-the-robots tournament while you're on your trip," Frankie said. "But she promised she'd help me program ours. We named it Boop the Destroyer."

I smiled at the thought of Trina maneuvering a robot called Boop the Destroyer. Frankie had invited Trina to the robotics club, and Trina was having fun with that too.

"Every time she tears another robot's limb off, she says, 'BEEP BOOP,'" Frankie said. "It's awesome."

"Hey, where's Lily?" Zora asked.

"She's doing some extra training during lunch," I said. "In the gym, over video. With her solo coming up, it's pretty intense for her."

"Are you sad you didn't get the solo?" Zora was always up front with her thoughts. "Like I was sooo jealous of Ariel when she got the lead."

"Don't put her on the spot!" Frankie admonished.

"Um," I said. "No, I'll answer. I mean, I definitely wanted the solo. I mean, I can't always dance the lead. Plus, my best friend on the team got it, so I'm happy for her! But yeah, it's complicated when there's only one spot."

"Could be worse," Frankie said seriously. "In robotics battle tournaments, if you don't get the lead, you get your metallic pieces ripped apart and flung outside the ring into the audience."

Nobody said anything for a second. Then we all laughed.

"Good point," Zora agreed.

As we were winding down, Courtney, another girl from the show, came over to our table. "Hey, Mrs. Elliott asked me to come tell you guys that the new makeup palettes came in if you guys want to go practice!"

"Yeah!" Almost everybody chimed in. I noticed Drew didn't, but when Courtney offered to make him up like a zombie, he jumped up with everybody else. I felt a little bit left out. It wasn't their fault—they had been super welcoming to me, and I loved that we still hung out. I just felt like lately, I had one foot in each world. I was a dancer who liked hanging out with the drama group, but didn't have time to be in the plays (actually, since I couldn't sing and I was new there, I wasn't sure I had the talent to be in the plays! But it was fun! So who knew?!).

"Okay, you guys have fun!" I told them.

"You have to come with us!" Zara insisted. "I know you don't have your own makeup palette, but that's okay—you can do someone's makeup or just come have fun."

She had a point. I jumped up and went with them backstage. There was a room that had a lot of makeup mirrors set up, and after everybody had gotten their makeup kits they all scrambled to get a seat.

"Harper, it's so nice to see you here," said Mrs. Elliott. "I wish I had a makeup kit for you, but we did a special order. You know, if you have time in your schedule, I'm going to be having an introduction to drama class, and you should join us!"

"I'd love to!" I said, and I meant it. At least I'd get to be part of drama during the school day and it wouldn't interfere with dance rehearsals! The makeup started in earnest. Courtney was making Drew into a zombie. Ariel was doing her own makeup to look glamorous and even more fabulous than she always does. Zora turn herself into . . . I wasn't sure, but it was very colorful!

"Harper, do you want to do my makeup?" Frankie asked. "I was going to try to turn myself into a robot, but I'm not good with makeup."

"How about I do something super-high-tech-looking?" I offered. After Frankie nodded, I had a great time finding silvery colors and metallic shimmers. I put silver and metallic blue on her eyes and a shimmery, sparkly powder all over her face, and then did her lips in a deep blue metallic-flecked matte lipstick. I loved to play with makeup at home, so this was really fun.

"Oh, wow—everyone look at Frankie!" Ariel pointed at us.

"I love this so much, and I don't even like makeup!" Frankie smiled. Everybody complimented each other on their makeup jobs and was appropriately scared of Drew's zombie look.

"AUHHHGGHH, I'm coming for you, Harper!" Drew lurched across the room toward me like a zombie, and I squealed and ran away. (Okay, I didn't run away too fast. Hee-hee.)

"If you need any help with the dances, let me know," I said.

"You focus on bringing home a win at nationals," Zora said. "Or at least a souvenir."

"I remember they do have great pizza," Drew said. "You think you could fit a pizza in your suitcase?"

"Could be messy." I laughed.

"Make us proud!" Zora said, dramatically fake-sniffing. "Our little Harper, all grown-up, going off the big city. To crush her enemies and destroy them!"

"Beep boop," I replied.

"*P*sst . . ."

     I heard the hiss, but I wasn't sure where it was coming from. Vanessa, a few chaperone parents, and the whole Squad were at the airport, seated at the gate for our New York City flight. We were facing one another in the two rows next to the window.

"Psst . . ."

There it was again. Everyone seated on either sides of me was either plugged into their music, busy chatting, or, like Lily right next to me, testing out their new neck pillows.

"Harper!" someone said in a loud whisper. "Over here!"

I looked across and saw Riley staring at me with wide eyes.

She was pointing her finger away from the window and miming something I couldn't make out.

I scrunched up my face. "Huh?"

She rolled her eyes, then grabbed her phone and started tapping on the screen. My phone buzzed right away. A text from Riley.

In front of you! Isn't that the actress that plays Trey Thompson's teacher on NYC High? Episode 3? I chuckled to myself. Riley's celebrity watch was starting sooner than I'd thought. If I didn't turn around and look where she was pointing, she'd keep bugging me. When I did, I definitely saw the resemblance. But no, it wasn't the same person. I shook my head.

She just shrugged her shoulders and started scanning the rest of the passengers for another sighting.

I grinned. It was a good thing I was sitting next to Lily on the flight. But I totally understood what Riley was feeling. Already, there was this excitement in the air. We were on our way to nationals! In New York City! I could hardly believe it.

I was pulling my DanceStarz rolling duffel up farther in line when I got a text.

Counting down to when you land!

Perfect timing. We're at the airport right now!
Eeeeeee!

She sent me a GIF of a dancing bagel, and I literally laughed out loud.

"What's so funny?" Lily asked, smiling.

"Just Eliza . . . Eliza-ing," I said, smiling at my screen. And then Eliza responded with a close-up of her actual face cracking up like the crying-laughing emoji. I cracked up, too. "She's super excited that I'm on my way."

"Oh," said Lily, sounding confused. "But didn't you say we'll be competing against your old dance studio? Isn't it weird?"

"Yeah, but we're not really mentioning that mostly," I told her.

"No, I mean . . . yeah, I can see how that would get awkward," Lily agreed. We pushed our luggage a bit forward together.

"Eliza's cool. I can't wait for you to meet her," I said.

Lily pulled out her earbuds from her bag. "I heard they'll keep us kind of busy touring New York in between our call times for the nationals," she said.

I panicked for a moment. "I hope not! I would be so bummed if I don't get a chance to hang out with Eliza. And everyone on my old squad. Well, not everyone will be there, because some of them stopped dancing or went somewhere else. But at least Eliza's there. I hope! If there's time!"

Lily looked surprised by my reaction. "I wouldn't worry too much about it. I'm sure everything will work out."

When I went back and took another look at Eliza's filtered face, I cracked up all over again and my worries disappeared.

Lily stood up, her carry-on bag on her shoulder. Was she sick of all my laughing?

"Where are you going?" I asked her.

"They called our group," she said. "Vanessa and the moms are looking for us."

That's when I looked around and realized that everyone is already making their way to board. How long had I been staring at my phone?

I scooped up my bag and followed Lily to the line.

Megan's mom started handing out our boarding passes. She had been holding them all, just in case.

"Lily, you're in seat 16A," she said, giving Lily her pass. "And, let's see, Harper is in seat 14C."

"But I thought I was sitting next to Lily," I said.

"Nope." Megan's mom double-checked our seat numbers. "It appears you're not."

I knew she was only stating facts, but I got the feeling she was enjoying my disappointment. It was hard not to imagine that when she looked so much like Megan, the person who'd always been extra challenging to me.

Lily and I exchanged a bummed-out look.

"But is there any way I can switch?" I plead.

Megan's mom shrugged. "You'll have to wait and see who you're both sitting with and ask them."

It was too late to go around asking everyone now. A few of us were already past the ticketing agent and walking down the jetway. Besides, I wanted to be a good sport and not a bratty baby about this. I decided to just be cool. And from the resolved look on Lily's face, I could tell she'd decided the same.

A few minutes later, as I followed the seat numbers down the aisle, I was in for a surprise when I saw Megan and Trina at row sixteen. Ack!

They both looked up at me, clearly wondering what I was doing there.

"Hey, guys," I said sheepishly. "I'm supposed to be sitting here, but I can totally swap with the person sitting next to Lily."

Megan peered up over the seat in front of her. She eyed Lily getting into row fourteen with . . .

I turned around to see who the person is. It was Megan's mom!

"Nope," said Megan. "I love my mom, but it's enough to have her chaperoning this whole trip. Not going to sit next to her if I don't have to!"

I puffed out a defeated sigh and gave Lily a sad wave. She waved back with a frown.

"You two will be sharing a room, so you'll have plenty of time to catch up later," said Trina.

"It's cool." I smiled, embarrassed that I'd dragged this on so long. At least I got the window seat.

Once I was buckled in, I texted Eliza to give her an update.

Boarded and so far, leaving on time.

It's a sunny and clear day here. Great day for a flight.

I hope so. ☺

I know so. ☼ 🚀

My grinning captured Megan's attention. She's seated next to me, hogging up both armrests. "Don't tell me you're texting Lily."

Trina looks at me and cracks up. "Oh, no. Is it like, *Hi, Lily. Do you sense me staring at the back of your head? How about now? Or now?*"

Megan snorts.

"As a matter of fact, I'm not texting her. I'm texting another friend."

"What other friend do you even have?" asked Megan, unironically.

"Eliza, from my old dance studio in Connecticut. She's excited I'm coming up," I explained.

"Wait," said Megan. "You said your old dance studio would be competing against us at nationals."

"Well, yeah, but they're still my friends," I said.

"They're our competitors," Megan shot back. "This happy little reunion better not interfere with nationals. Eliza is going to be going up against us, so I hope you remember that."

The sour taste in her warning lingered. But a moment later our plane started zooming down the runway for takeoff and Megan suddenly looked nervous.

"You okay?" Trina asked Megan.

"Yeah, I'm fine. I just— Oop!" The plane jostled its way down the runway, and Megan shut her eyes.

"You're a nervous flyer?" I asked.

"No, pfft," she said. Then she opened one eye. "Okay, maybe a little. Whatever."

We hit a little bump, and Megan shrieked.

"Megan, we're still on the ground," I told her. "And don't worry, we'll distract you when we're actually up in the air."

She winced and clutched the armrests tighter. "Promise?"

"We promise," Trina and I responded.

It ended up being actually a fun flight. We played cards and *Would You Rather?*, and I learned something new about both of them (Megan would rather go waterskiing, Trina snow skiing; Megan would rather have an extra eye, and Trina would rather have two noses). And we also managed to get Megan through the worst of the turbulence, even though I had a feeling I would have nail marks when she dug into my arm after a particularly big bump. Bonding accomplished!

As we peered down on skyscrapers on our approach to LaGuardia Airport in New York, I was all too happy to point out any landmarks I recognized.

"There's the Statue of Liberty! And one of the big bridges—I always forget which one is which!" I pointed them out to Megan. I think she actually had tears in her eyes from joy. (Or maybe from relief we were almost on the ground.)

I couldn't wait to show everyone New York.

I was baaaack!

J was grateful passenger vans didn't have assigned seats. It was so nice to be sitting next to Lily again. As we were all transported from the airport in Queens to the hotel in Manhattan, we were able to take in the first New York City sights from the second row.

While the van weaved through the crowded highway, Lily commented on different things out her window.

"The highway is so narrow! So many cars!" she said.

"So fast. So many turns. I think I'm going to throw up," Riley said, holding her mouth.

"You get used to it after a while," I answered.

"How do I find my seat belt in this thing?" Riley twisted and turned in her seat next to Lily and me.

"You're already wearing your seat belt," Lily pointed out, grinning. Riley was acting as jumpy as Megan had during in-flight turbulence.

I pulled out my phone and snapped a picture of the highway sign that read MANHATTAN and MIDTOWN TUNNEL and texted it off with a quick note.

Lily looked at me as if she knew exactly what I was up to.

"Eliza again?" she asked.

I smiled at her. "No. I sent it to my parents."

"Oh. Okay." Lily looked almost relieved. "Sorry for assuming."

"Don't be too impressed," Trina told Lily. "She wasn't texting Eliza, because Eliza already knows we're here. As soon as we touched down, she was texting her our status."

"Oh, come on, you would be excited about going back home to meet your old dance crew too," I said.

"Uh, no," Megan said. "Mine is the Bells. Not excited to see them ever. Not excited to see Isabella in New York, either."

Hmm. She had a point there. But Eliza was different.

"Isabella!" Trina shrank in her seat. Even the mention of

her name still weirded Trina out. Isabella was intimidating. "She was—"

The van abruptly swerved and Trina lost her train of thought. She didn't continue her statement, for which I was grateful. She just grabbed her headset and plugged into her soothing music. I liked the zoned-out Trina much better.

"You're right, I'm sorry," said Lily. "I would be excited about going back to my old gymnastics team too. I mean, who wouldn't be eager to see a good friend again?"

"I really think you and Eliza will get along," I said, patting Lily's knee.

"I'm excited to meet her," she replied cheerfully.

"Great!" I said. It seemed silly that everyone was so focused on Eliza, like I was going to go and give her all our secrets or something. I would love for both of my dance worlds to get along.

"We'll be there in no time," I said, back to the reassuring mode I'd used for Megan on the flight over. "Check it out!" I nudged Riley. "Look! We are getting closer."

The van climbed a hilly part of the highway, and when it reached the peak, the gleaming New York City skyline came into view. The skyscrapers reflected the bright midday sun, and we all gasped and cheered when we saw it.

"New York City, here we come!" Megan shouted from the front seat, throwing up her arms as high as they could go in a low-ceiling vehicle, still relieved she'd survived the flight.

"Whoop!" hollered Lily.

"The Squad takes Manhattan!" I shouted, grabbing Lily and Trina's hands and throwing them up with mine.

Everyone cheered and took videos of our mini celebration. And the closer we got, the less concerned Riley became about the dicey city driving.

We were so pumped by the time we reached the fashionably old-world hotel, no one was ready to stay inside. As we gathered in the marble-walled elevator bank we began to sound like a bunch of toddlers, trying to convince the chaperones to let us go out. "Can we? Please, can we?"

"Fine!" Vanessa held up her hands and shouted above the whining. "All those interested in a predinner stroll through Rockefeller Center, meet me back down here in twenty minutes."

We jumped up and down and squealed, not caring how cheesy we were acting. We scored another victory when we crowded out our chaperones and nabbed an elevator all to ourselves. We all were silly dancing when the elevator doors opened. And Isabella was inside. Ack!

"Looks like the cool quotient of New York City just went down a few notches," Isabella said in a fake-playful way the moment the elevator doors closed us in together. "JK. Gee whiz, that was some cheerful arrival."

"Oh, Isabella. I didn't know you were staying at the same hotel," Megan said, obviously mortified but trying to hide it.

"Most of the dance teams are staying in this hotel, because the nationals are held in the grand ballroom downstairs. But you just got here, so how could you have known?" She talked like she'd been here weeks or months longer than we had. "I've been bumping into newcomers like you from lots of dance studios."

"It's not all of our first time visiting New York," Megan says, reaching for me and nudging me forward. "We've got a local girl ready to show us around."

That was not at all what I'd expected, so I got a bit tongue-tied now that I was put on the spot.

"Oh, really?" she said. "That's handy—you know, we were just wondering what subway stops are by here. We've been taking car service, but I might go underground in order go to downtown for something different. So, subway? I'm sure you know that off the top of your head."

Had I just stepped into some elevator quiz reality show?

I looked up at the cameras and wondered if there was a live studio audience watching somewhere.

"But if you don't know—" challenged Isabella.

"Oh, she knows," Megan insisted.

Oh, I didn't know.

But maybe I was off the hook. *Ding!* We'd reached our floor, but everyone was still staring, waiting, hoping for me to get it right or wrong.

"Our floor," I said quickly, and exited first. I swallowed hard, hoping the Squad followed me off, leaving Isabella on the elevator. I took a few paces onto our floor and breathed easier knowing the pressure was off.

I turned around to chat with the Squad. "Whew, that was . . ."

Isabella standing there. On our floor. Waiting. On my answer!

Seriously?

"What a coincidence." She crossed her arms. "We happen to be staying on the same floor. So, subway station? Miss Know Everything About New York City."

Megan and Riley looked like they wanted to Google the answer telepathically. Lily and I exchanged a look that confirmed we both thought this was bonkers.

I've been to New York plenty of times, but never on my own. I mean, who really knows all the subway stations? I came in from Connecticut! I was always following my parents, some other older relative, or a chaperone. That's when it popped into my head: the lyrics to the jazzy song I danced to at my old studio last year. *Nothing betta/Than Rockefeller/Here's what to do/ Take the B, D, F, M, and Q . . .*

"The B, D, F, M, and Q," I said, my heart thumping. Rockefeller Center, where we were!

Isabella's thumbs rapid-tapped her cell screen, then she paused for a second before reporting: "Okay, you're right."

"DanceStarz are always right," boasted Megan. "Come on, girls. We have to be ready for Harper's city tour in fifteen minutes."

We pivoted with sass and headed down the hall, leaving the Energii dancers standing there to get swallowed up by our chaperones, who spilled out of the next elevator.

8

The Squad, Megan's and Riley's moms, and Vanessa walked the wide city streets at the height of rush hour. It was a chilly day, and there's a clashing of sounds, smells, and even—for Riley— tastes. She got really excited just stepping out on the street. The first thing we saw was a street vendor.

"My first street hot dog," Riley said before gnawing off a mouthful. "You guys are going to regret not ordering one for yourselves."

"You didn't even order that one for yourself," says Megan. "Harper ordered it for you."

Trina giggled. It's true. Riley had been so caught up over how to phrase her order, and what local terms she should use when ordering, that she'd shied away from it altogether.

"Oh, you know you wanted one too," Riley said cheerfully. Megan's mother had muttered that it was disgusting to order off the street, so Megan didn't get one. She scowled. We snapped a pic of Riley holding up her hard-earned hot dog, a ginormous stone fountain in the background.

It's funny: As we joined the crowds, it all came back to me. I zigzagged my way through the sidewalks full of fast-walking people, tourists with their cameras and fanny packs, making a hole for the rest of the crew to follow behind safely. I learned these moves from my dad, who used to work in the city. When we'd meet him here for lunch, he would take long strides and tunnel his way through any slow-moving mob of people, and we'd be running to keep up. He knew all the shortcuts and the best eateries.

I also knew what was in store for us that was crazy exciting. Something that people from all over the world came especially to see.

"There are so many people!" Lily said.

"It's that time of year for tourists," I said. "Just wait."

We cross the street, and . . . oh! THE TREE! Rockefeller Plaza is the site of the world's most famous Christmas tree. It had recently been lit, and we all oohed and aahed over it.

"'The tree has been lit annually for over eighty years,'" Lily read off a sign. "'More than one hundred million people visit every year.' Whoa."

"Picture time!" The moms whipped out their cameras and had us shuffle as close to the tree as we could. "Say 'cheese'!"

We walked around and saw the famous skating rink, where people were ice-skating in circles, doing tricks—and falling down laughing. I remembered my parents taking me to ice-skate every few years as a special holiday treat. We looked at some of the incredible, lit-up holiday window displays. Being back there brought on nice memories I hadn't thought of in a while.

"It's nice to see you so happy," Lily said. "I can tell you're loving this."

"What about you?" I asked. "Are you having fun so far?

"So far, so good," said Lily. "But if that changes, I've got the best local guide to turn up the fun."

"At your service." I curtsy with an exaggerated leg tuck.

"I have to admit it is colder than I thought." Riley's mother shivered. She had dressed for style, in a thin wool coat. "I underestimated this."

Florida people, I thought. We'd been told to bundle up, and I'd worn my last year's black ski jacket, furry boots, and thick purple gloves. Also my favorite pale lilac hat with a white fluffy pom-pom on the top. But I realized they didn't have any need for them usually—so why would they have it on hand?

"I vote for some . . . shopping!" Megan's mom said. We all cheered.

"There are lots of stores around here," I said. "Bigger versions of what we have in Florida. Also, over there is a shop where we'd always buy thick leggings and hats and warm tech stuff!"

We all split up. Those who needed warmer clothes (Riley's mom, Riley, and Lily) and the rest of us who went to the trendy store next door to look at cute sweaters and boots and accessories. Megan bought a sparkly skirt, and Trina got a bracelet. They were cute, and I was tempted, but I was saving my money for the stores downtown that we didn't have in Florida.

"Ah, much better." Riley came out wearing a cute brown teddy-bear-style coat.

"Love the coat," we told her. Then Lily followed behind.

I had to laugh. Lily was bundled up in a puffer jacket, with huge green earmuffs and a huge scarf wrapped around her head. You could only see her eyes peeking through.

"Lily, are you in there?" I leaned in.

Then we went into the store that was attached to a television studio. It was so fun for everyone to see shirts and gifts that was from some of our favorite shows and know that some of them were even being filmed right upstairs in the Rockefeller Center building studios!

"Girls, we're going to stop in here to pick up a few souvenirs," said Vanessa, before walking into a tourist trap of a store with our other two chaperones. "Trina really wants a snow globe."

"For my collection," Trina said.

"You have a snow globe collection?" Riley asked.

"I'm starting one now," Trina said brightly. "We don't get snow in Florida, so I am going to get one here!"

Lily and I decided to wait right outside the store.

My phone rang. Eliza. On video chat!

"Hello from Rockefeller Center!" I answered.

"Oh my gosh, then that is you?" Eliza squealed over the traffic noise.

"On the screen? Yes! Did you not mean to call me?"

"No—I mean yes. I mean no, that's not what I meant. Did you just curtsy? Because there's a girl across the street from us that looks just like you."

I started waving and laughing boisterously.

"Yes! Yes, it's you! I'm crossing the street right now!"

I watched as Eliza's long blond hair practically floated behind her, she was running so fast across the crosswalk toward me! She was wearing a navy coat, buckled up over black tights and flats.

"Trina is happy with the shiny things in there," Megan said as she came out with Riley. Then they stood like astonished statues as Eliza ran from the crosswalk and and we hugged and squealed and shouted and hugged again.

"Wow, I didn't realize you'd be staying this close to the venue. We're just leaving rehearsal at the dance studio," said Eliza.

"We have ours tomorrow."

"Ahem!" Megan cleared her throat.

"Oh, I almost forgot. . . ." I turn to the Squad. "Eliza, meet my new Squad members, Lily, Megan, Riley—and here comes Trina."

"Hi, everyone!" said Eliza, giving the group a big smile. "I hope you're looking out for my girl. She's very special to me."

I take a look at the Squad, but they're barely smiling.

"Of course we are," Megan said finally. "She's special to us, too."

"Speaking of special," Eliza continues. "I've got a special treat tomorrow. I'll pick you up at lunch."

"Awesome, I'll see you then!" I said.

Lily's eyebrows go up, and Megan exchanges a look with Riley and Trina.

Eliza gave everyone a friendly wave. "It was nice to meet you guys! I hope we get to hang out a little this week."

"Isn't she great? Isn't this whole trip the coolest?" I ask.

"Cooler than the rink," Megan said.

*T*he next morning, after a yummy New York breakfast—including bagels, of course—we walked to the rented studios assigned to most of the nationals competitors. We had a specific private room and practice time. We had to get there early and use our time wisely, because that would that be our only private run-through while we're here. Tomorrow we'd be running through a sort-of dress rehearsal at the hotel ball-room, making sure we all knew our designated performance times, and marking everything. And there, people were invited to stay and watch from the audience.

"This is it, girls," Vanessa said when we entered the sunlight-drenched white space. We're a few floors above street level and out the windows are buildings that look made for black-and-white photography.

It's one thing to have the choreography down, but it's another to adapt it to the space you're rehearsing or performing in. Vanessa believes a choreographed work can change its look and feel depending on the setting. And from the sound of it, she definitely thinks this dance comes to life a little differently here in this studio. Who's to say how it will play out once we hit the competition stage at nationals.

But that's our job. To make adjustments on the spot and remember them.

"That last move on the 'and four' isn't working anymore," says Vanessa. "Let's instead reverse the step and see if that works better."

We twist the opposite way with the "and four" and then look to our instructor, whose face says it all.

"Yup, that's it. Remember that change. Let's do it again!"

Vanessa drilled into us all the new choreography changes, until they became second nature to us. Lily performed with flawless extension because she's the most flexible one on the team. Trina's trademark footwork skills were at their peak. Riley's signature facials could not and would not fail to energize the audience. Megan owned her tricks and overall awesomeness like nobody's business. And I managed to make my fiercest leaps and turns look easy. After a quick bite to eat—thank goodness for the downstairs deli—we went in one at a time to rehearse our solos.

"Come in," Vanessa greeted me when it was time to work on my solo. I left the other girls in the warm-up room, where we had been listening to music and doing our stretches and conditioning. It was a cool-down room that we all appreciated having access to after the nonstop rehearsing. And, knowing that we nailed the group performance and switched to a solos mind-set, everyone had kind of retreated to their own individual bubbles. There was less talking and joking around. It was every dancer for herself.

"Ready?" Vanessa asked me as I placed my bag down in one corner and peeled out of my gold, white, and pink jacket and matching track pants.

In the months since I'd joined DanceStarz Academy, Vanessa had become someone I totally admired. She may be tough at times like this, but she has a way of recognizing your strengths and pushing you to reach further, aim higher, go harder.

"Ready!" I nodded, focused and pumped.

My solo was a lyrical dance with intricate footwork. At

first I was mortified that Vanessa would pick something with tricky footwork. She knew what a hard time I had learning how to perform like this without looking like I'm counting in my head and concentrating on every step.

When I first joined her dance studio, she got Trina to meet with me after hours for the extra help I desperately needed. Never mind how embarrassing that was for me to acknowledge at first. The last thing I wanted to do as a dancer was come across robotic. Especially at an epic event like nationals. For the few moments following her announcement of our scheduled solos, it felt like Vanessa was trying to sabotage me.

"Is there any way I can perform a different type of choreography at nationals?" I'd stayed behind to ask her at the time.

"I wouldn't give you anything you couldn't handle," she'd answered. "And I believe you can do this. Besides, the judges in New York will award a routine like this higher technical points, which will put you in the running for the top spots."

As amazing as that sounded, there was more than top spots on the line. Scouts from the most coveted summer dance programs would be in the audience at nationals, recruiting standout performers. A strong showing meant an invitation to one of those career-making programs. This would be a dream come true. I knew this was the same for Megan and Eliza, too.

"I believe you can do this." Those words echoed in my mind as I went through the moves over and over—sometimes tripping up a little, but always trying again.

By the time I had to give up the room, I was sweaty, exhausted, and worn-out, but I was ready and confident.

We were all happy to get back to our hotel room and hit the showers.

"You can go first," I told Lily as we both stood with arms full of shampoo, soap, and body lotion.

"No, you go ahead," she said. "I know you have your friend coming to pick you up soon."

Oh, yeah. Lily had overheard Eliza asking me to lunch. I had been sort of afraid to remind her, so a part of me was glad I didn't have to.

"I wish you could come too, but I'm not sure what she's got planned."

Was it rude not to insist the Squad come along—or at least Lily? But no, they had to understand that I needed alone time with my friend. Besides, Eliza's mom was authorized to take me out for a couple of hours. I didn't think she could just take anyone else along with us, unless one of the mom chaperones joined us.

"No, it's okay—really," says Lily. "I wouldn't want to miss

where Vanessa will take us after lunch. Riley thinks Vanessa set up a fun surprise."

Was Lily jealous?

She's just a little stressed, I said to myself. It had been an intense day, and everyone was starting to get nervous about nationals. Yup, just needs some time.

"Is this place even real?" Eliza and I were in front of Cupcake Queen, already smelling all of the sugary goodness that was waiting for us inside.

I walked into the cupcake bakery with my jaw hanging. It was like we'd been transported to inside a painting. The walls were all murals of cool cityscapes. Without overdoing it, the splashes of color all complemented one another in a way I wouldn't have expected.

And behind the glass counter were rows and rows of deliciously colorful cupcakes. These were no ordinary cupcakes. They had magical powers.

"I knew you'd love it," said Eliza. Her mom grabbed a seat in the far corner. She'd been nice enough to come with us, since we couldn't go by ourselves, and had brought a book along so Eliza and I could hang out.

"I forgot just how much you know about me," I said.

"Of course! Just because you're the new girl in Florida doesn't mean you're the new girl here."

The truth of Eliza's simple statement struck me. That's totally right. Unlike in Florida, I had history here. I had a past people were familiar with. I had a track record. A pretty cool one, especially when it came to dance.

We ordered swirly cupcakes with chocolate frosting, and grabbed seats at a bright two-seater table.

"Mmm, this is the perfect dessert after the pizza we had," I declared between delicious bites.

It had been a while since I'd visited one of those famous NYC pizzeria shops that were so common, especially downtown. During our lunch, we'd posted our selfies with floating emoji pizzas streaking down our pic. It seemed Eliza and I had been cracking up at every little thing ever since.

But now it seemed the conversation was getting a bit more real-life.

Eliza took a long sip of her water. "So, tell me what's been up with you." Eliza leaned in closer, as if she's asking me to tell her my deepest secrets. "Are you loving Florida?"

"Yup, it's a pretty place to live," I casually answer. "I don't think I'll ever get sick of seeing palm trees."

"Good." Eliza smiled cheerily. She took another bite of her

cupcake. "What about your new studio? How's that going? Looks like you've made some pretty cool friends there."

"Yeah, I got lucky." I smiled a little wider. "With Lily, especially. She's super supportive."

Eliza nodded. "We all need someone like that. Remember how hard we used to push each other?"

I shake my head. "How can I forget?"

She laughed. "Remember that time we couldn't get our double-timed move down fast enough? We must've tried it over a million times until we got it."

I winced at the memory. "That was pretty intense. Lily is a different kind of supportive, though."

Eliza scrunched up her face. "How do you mean?"

"Well, she's more cheerleader than coach," I said. "She reminds me to have fun, which is nice."

"Sure, fun is important. But . . ." Eliza shrugged. "No judgment. Just wondering if you're staying challenged like you did when you were here. Remember what Ms. Fiona used to say to us—"

"'Can't get too comfy, girls!'" we say at the same time with that same cracked voice Ms. Fiona used to speak in. We chuckle at the memory.

Being here with Eliza, reminded about what used to be

important to me, was eye-opening. In some ways, I had changed a lot. In others, though, I hadn't.

"I'm still the same go-hard dancer you remember," I replied, wiping my mouth of any lingering green icing.

"Good, because we've got to dig deep at the nationals," Eliza said. "The scouts are coming, and this is the time to start making choices."

"Yeah, I want to make a good impression on them and see how far I can take it." I said I actually hadn't admitted that to anyone else yet, but I realized how excited I was at the possibility of going for one of the summer programs.

"Well, this is the epicenter of dance right here," she said. "If you can make it here, you can make it anywhere."

I recognized the lyrics to that famous old song, so I started singing the rest. "It's up to you—"

Eliza joined in. "New York, New York!"

We cracked up all over again. Just like old times!

10

Zzzzzzzzzzzz.

I shut off the buzzing alarm on my cell phone and willed myself awake a half hour earlier than I'd intended. Careful not to wake Lily in the queen-size bed beside mine, I grabbed my secret stash of fruit I'd brought home from our dinner last night. As gross as it sounded, the best place to do this quietly was the bathroom, for sure.

I shut the door behind me and cut up the pear and apple I had grabbed as best as I could. Next I took the clean fruit to the nook where the coffeemaker and extra cups were stored. Even though this area was in the tiny hallway entrance to our hotel room, it was still tucked away and private enough that I wouldn't be seen if Lily suddenly woke up.

As I worked on my secret Operation Cheer Up Lily project, I guessed salvaging this fruit was the one good thing about our team dinner last night. Vanessa and the chaperones did most of the talking. Well, actually, Vanessa mostly did the listening. She was great at head nods and reactions at just the right time, when I'm pretty sure she was not paying one hundred percent attention. But nevertheless, now I knew all there was to know about Megan's mother and Riley's mom, including that they play tennis together and their views on social media monitoring (there should be more), legal driving ages (it should be raised), and sunglasses styles.

If Trina and Megan were embarrassed by any overheard revelations, I couldn't tell. Had it not be for their chewing, they would've been scowling the entire night. And Lily just wore a nonstop mopey face. Riley was lost in her phone, researching whether Trey Thomspon was in town and how to track his every move. I seemed to have been the only person feeling totally normal and even happy. Everyone was a little more on edge than usual. And I wanted to at least lighten the mood for my favorite person on the team.

I knew Lily was a huge fan of art. My sister, Hailey, had

gone through a celebrity chef phase, and I'd been forced to watch every reality competition and browse through every recipe in search for what her idol chef called the "sweet-savory-silly triple threat"—a delicious meal with a playful twist.

In the process, Hailey picked up a million and one ways to make cool food designs, and I figured what better way to turn Lily's frown upside down by combining her two favorite things: food and art! For this one, I was making a leaping dancer. I'd hardly thought I could get away with undertaking anything so fancy-sounding months ago. But Hailey's boot camp had made a liar out of me.

I made the slices of apple and pear look like a little human stick figure. With the strips of apple skin peel, I personalized it to make it look like she was flying as she leapt into the air. I'd saved my chocolate chip cookie from dessert as well. I broke it to get to an intact chocolate chip. That would make a good hair accessory. With all the crumbs left, I sprinkled some along the apple and pear slices I'd arranged on the plate in pretty patterns.

Just as I was wiping the corners of the plate clean, like I'd watched chefs on TV do plenty of times, Lily started stirring. As I quickly wrapped a plastic knife in a napkin, the room brightened up. Lily had drawn the curtains to let the morning sun in.

My jazz hands were more like jazz *hand*, but I did it with extra flair. "Good morning!" I said in the most singsong and cheery voice as possible. Startled, Lily whipped around, but when her eyes fell on the plate, she smiled from ear to ear.

"Oh my gosh, is that supposed to be me?" she squealed as best as she could with a croaky morning voice.

"Who else has leg extensions like that?" I grinned.

"Aw, that's so sweet of you . . . literally." She accepted the plate and checked out my food art. "I love it!"

"I'm so glad you do!" I couldn't stop smiling. "Go ahead, take a bite."

"It's too cute to eat!"

Lily was beaming like the rays of sun filtering in our room. Granted, our window was facing a side street—and whenever you're talking New York, that was like being in a canyon. But it was way brighter than with the curtains drawn.

If this small gesture left Lily less mopey than at dinner last night, then I'd consider that a victory.

"Oooh, wait!" Lily put the plate down on one corner of a crowded desk. "Let me take a pic of it."

I cracked up at all the snaps she took from what seemed like every angle.

"I think that's enough." I laughed.

"I want to copy this when I get back home. My parents should totally go with this type of presentation at the fro-yo shop."

"Oh, yeah. Maybe for birthday parties?" I pointed to her.

"Right? Or for the younger dancers after recitals." She pointed back.

"That's brilliant!" I lobbed a throw pillow at her in my version of the happy slap.

"I know!" She hurled the pillow right back at me.

I backed up to the bed as nonchalantly as possible as I spoke. "And we can get Hailey to help come out with more artsy ideas because she knows a . . . TON!" I tossed a large pillow with extra oomph.

I barely had time to crack up at how spot-on my launch was, when that same pillow muffled my laugh as it boomeranged back to my nose. And with that, the pillow wars were declared. The arm strength and lung capacity it took to fling pillows, stuffed animals, and towels at each other while laughing was epic. At the end of it all, we lay on a cushiony heap, out of breath and holding our splitting sides.

"I'm finally hungry enough to eat food art without guilt," she said. We cracked up again.

A few more foodie photos and lots of happy bites later, Lily and I took rush showers. We were dressed, packed, and picking up the pillow and towel mess when there was a knock on our door.

"Let's go, girls," said Riley's mom's muffled voice. "Time to head out."

Our commute wasn't far at all. All we had to do was take the elevator down from the lobby restaurant where we had breakfast. But thankfully, we were all very far from the mood most of us were in the night before. We couldn't loosen up.

Megan's and Riley's moms made casual small talk with ease. But Vanessa was the only one who seemed deep in thought and a little bit distracted.

"Girls, a moment, please," Vanessa said as we waited in the elevator lobby after breakfast. We paused from our playful banter and turned our attention to her. Vanessa's words were even-toned. She kept her hands rigid and fingers together, and it seemed like she was using them to wall in her words. "We need to be sharper than ever today. Not just onstage, but when we're watching other performers, when we're backstage, when we're anywhere in between. Okay? Your professionalism is of utmost importance, because it helps show organizers keep everything flowing properly."

We nodded and stole glances at one another, the seriousness of competing on this level hitting us on an even deeper level than before. The group and solo competitions would be streaming online, and today was set up so that the organizers could run those programs. The best part about today was that each team would get their turn to feel out the stage.

"That said"—Vanessa drew out a sneaky smile, her hands back to their relaxed state—"have fun out there and remind everyone why they first started dancing in the first place!"

We whooped and cheered our way onto the waiting elevator. When the sliding doors opened up to the lower level, the thumping sound of dance music wafted from the grand ballroom up the wide, carpeted hall to greet us.

We headed toward the music, aiming for the rectangular registration table, where three people were seated, each one addressing a line of people waiting to consult with them.

One look at the grandeur of it all, the top-tier dancers milling around, and Megan's mom was overcome. I mean, she totally got all starry-eyed emoji on us. "Here we are, at the world-class arena I've always dreamed of performing in."

"Really, Mom? I never knew this was a dream of yours," said Megan, surprised.

Yup. That makes perfect sense, I thought to myself.

Megan's mom snaps out of her starry daydream. "Don't be

silly," she said, exasperated. "I was talking about you. *You've* always imagined this."

"Um, no, we all heard you say—"

"Trina, darling, come and take a look at this," said Riley's mom, trying to smooth over the awkwardness, leading her to a display lining one side of the wall.

"Oooh!" said Trina, wide-eyed. "This is . . . wow."

But this wasn't just about distracting Trina—the display was legit amazing. We all walked over, totally drawn by the neatly arranged display of autographed portraits.

It was a pop-up museum collection about dance legends. And not just about dance legends, but the ones who'd performed here at this very competition!

"I'll go sign us in and pick up our passes," said Vanessa before making her way to the line that had formed in front of the registration table's A–F sign.

We were so grateful for the extra time to study the wall of fame.

"Look!" Riley pointed to one vintage image of a dance troupe from the 1950s. "Is that the same Bailar Studio in Florida that we know?"

Our huddle around the white card got tighter as we read the fine-print description of the image.

"That's bananas," said Megan.

"That's amazing," Lily said breathlessly, clearly touched by what she was seeing.

"Whoa" was all I could add. Coming face-to-face with the sense of how many greats had performed on this stage kind of had us all at a loss for words. But in a good way.

Suddenly, I felt like being dancers could change the world.

Vanessa had to wave her hands in front of our faces to help us realize she was ready to take us to the performance hall. There, we took our seats among the dancers already camped out in the row of cushioned seats. And we sat there watching producers call teams by name backstage and then eventually onto the stage, where they, without revealing their performance moves, loosely ran through aspects of their performance. Things like how far apart to stand and how far forward and far back everyone could go were worked out.

After close to two hours, we were finally called backstage and shown our shared dressing area. It was huge compared to what we were used to.

"This is nice," said Vanessa, nodding her head.

Riley snapped a pic every time Vanessa and the producer's backs were turned. I could tell the *act professional* speech Vanessa had given was on her mind.

Next, the producer walked briskly to the stage, and we had to trot to keep up. As instructed, we remained offstage until we were given the signal.

"Go!"

And just like that, it was our turn to be onstage, examining the floors, the audience view, the feel of it. We could see the waiting dance teams chatting to each other in the audience. A few took interest in us, maybe because they recognized the name of our dance studio, or they were hoping for a glimpse of our routine. After our time was up, we were led back to the audience, where we would wait another two hours for our solo dance runs.

But throughout it all, the boost we got from the pop-up museum stayed super high. More than ever, I was ready to compete and show everyone what I was made of!

11

Who knew Vanessa was so sneaky and secretive? After dropping off our bags, freshening up and having lunch together, Vanessa announced she had a surprise for us. She didn't even drop us a hint. All she did was lead us out of the hotel. Even though Vanessa wasn't saying a word, that didn't stop us from getting into a guessing game.

"I hope it's a Trey Thompson meet and greet!" wished Riley, squealing like the screech of a subway train brakes we could hear through the sidewalk grates underneath our feet.

"Barneys?" Megan asked hopefully.

"You want a meet and greet with the purple dinosaur?" Trina asked earnestly.

"If I have to explain that, you're not ready to learn what it is." Megan rolled her eyes.

"It's some high-end department store," I explained to Trina. "My mom said she walked in one day and nearly passed out after peeking at the price tags."

Lily sounded confident with her guess. "Madame Tussauds wax museum. I read that it's every tourist's must-see spot, plus it's supposed to be pretty close to our hotel."

We looked to Vanessa, who was texting someone as we waited for the light to change.

"You'll have to wait and see," she said, giving secret smiles to the moms, who apparently were in on the big plan.

We up a side street for what seems like ages, but we finally come to the biggest intersection, right ahead of us.

The flashing lights, the ginormous faces on the billboards, the HD jumbotrons.

"TIMES SQUARE!" a couple of Squad members called out in disbelief.

Riley immediately started taking photos of the sights, of our amazement. Then she gave her phone to Megan's mom and jumped into a group shot with us.

"The Squad in Times Square!" Riley shouted as Megan's mom snapped away.

This was where everything happened. I'd never come here enough with my family. They were big on avoiding the congestion on this area's streets and sidewalks.

"Every time I come here, I always feel like I'm in the center of the universe," said Trina.

"I know! It's like everybody in the entire world is here," I said.

"Thank you, Vanessa," said Lily. "I can't believe I'm actually here, in the place I've seen in movies a zillion times before."

"This is such a cool surprise!" shouted Megan, who was showing the most enthusiasm for New York since she got here.

"You're welcome, but this isn't the surprise." Vanessa winked. Still, we dived into the frenzied energy of the broad strip, where two main avenues intersect and explode into a loud, bright, flashing epicenter.

We stood on the bleachers, which were in front of the famous TKTS booth (where you could buy discount Broadway tickets). Tons of people were standing or sitting there, but we found an empty spot and snapped away, taking in the view. Even the moms got in on the fun. After we were done, we joined the herd of humans migrating across the wide street when we got the green light.

We found ourselves on a quieter side street. "Here we are!"

said Vanessa, holding open a nondescript white door leading to a flight of stairs.

We'd given up asking for clues by then. And besides, we were still buzzing from our cool Times Square photo shoot. Even Megan seemed a little giddy.

That's when we saw the sign at the top of the stairs: THE ALEXIS ALMA STUDIOS.

"No way!" I shouted.

Alexis Alma was only this super-awesome choreographer and dancer who took hip-hop dance to top stages around the world. She was a legend who got her start dancing in the most popular music videos back when our parents were our age.

"Yes way!" Vanessa smiled from ear to ear. "Courtesy of the organizers of our competition, we get to not only visit, but take a class with their star instructors!"

"OMG!" We all shrieked.

"Okay, okay." Vanessa was smiling, even as she tried to settle us down. "Let's go in there calm and composed."

"Yeah, hurry, because more people are coming in behind us and we want to get the best spots!" said Megan's mom.

Fifteen minutes later, we were front row center in a big dance studio. A bunch of the other teams were there, too. They seemed just as nervous and excited as we were.

Wow. There were about one hundred of us in there. Plus, there was plenty of space for all the chaperones to sit and chill in the back of the room. I'd only ever seen these warehouse-size studios on those super-polished YouTube videos showcasing the latest dance crazes. I wonder if they used this studio in the videos.

I had to ask Lily, who loved those videos as much as I did. She was standing next to me but looked lost in thought.

I leaned an inch over to my left. "Psst! The dance videos we love watching. I bet they're filmed here!"

Lily broke out of her thoughts and grinned. We grabbed each other's hands and did one last mini squeal, until one after another, a man and a woman's voices echoed out.

"Hello, everyone!" said the man.

"Waddup, people!" the woman bellowed.

"Welcome, welcome!"

They were both now standing in front of us, dressed in white tees, joggers, and sneakers. The mirror behind them reflected all our faces. They introduced themselves as Jackie and Miguel.

"Please take a seat for now while we talk your ear off," Jackie joked.

We all laughed.

"We heard you all have a major event coming up, and we applaud you for making it this far," shouted Jackie, beaming and throwing her hands in the air.

Everyone erupted into a mini celebration, cheering for ourselves and one another. It felt great to shout extra loud with my dance crew. The Squad and I all high-fived one another .

"Now, we know a thing or two about competition," said Miguel, "and it can be pretty nerve-wracking. We hope to offer you a fun break from your competition worries—and give you a taste of New York City dance lessons."

Lily, Riley, Trina, and I stole glances at each other, smiling.

"Okay, guys, let's go! Warm-up time!" Jackie called out.

We all go to the center of the room, where we go through a series of mini cardio—including lots of sit-ups and push-ups to get the blood pumping.

After we were done, Miguel jumped up and down as if revving up his energy even more. He gestured for us to get up and do the same. "So, let's pop, rock, and lock when that hip-hop beat drops."

The music started, and we all got moving in all different types of styles. And then both instructors did their jumping thing again. When the entire studio was jumping too, they started showing us a hip-hop routine that we all followed.

They broke down each move to its simplest form, so we were able to catch on quicker than I'd thought. It was great.

For the next half hour, we lost ourselves in the rhythm and rhymes of hip-hop, using our arms, legs, shoulders, and even our hands. Even the chaperones were out of their seats, jamming with all their hearts.

We almost complained out loud when Jackie turned down the music.

"All right, now we usually like to bring up a few dancers to show what they've learned," said Miguel. Too many hands shot up, which got everyone laughing.

"How about we bring up the winners of our New York pop quiz?" said Jackie. "And no Googling, people."

Everyone laughed again, but this time it was way more authentic. We were already fans of Jackie and Miguel.

"Name all five—"

My arm went up like I was trying to touch the ceiling. I'd lived in this area long enough what people were talking about when they said the number five.

"Manhattan, Brooklyn, Queens, the Bronx, and Staten Island." I shouted, cracking up.

"I didn't even finish! The five boroughs—and she is correct!" Everyone laughed at Miguel's faux-shocked face.

The Squad cheered for me, patting me on the back. Jackie gestured for me to join them up front.

"Wow. Okay, looks like we've got a local here," she said. "Where are you from?"

"Connecticut!" I said it without thinking. It wasn't until I saw the Squad all look at one another like they missed something had I realized that it sounded like I wasn't planning to rep for Florida or DanceStarz. But my Squad knew I loved them, so I figured no harm done.

Jackie and Miguel were running away with the whole Connecticut shout-out.

Miguel pointed at the Squad in the front row. "Are you all from Connecticut too?"

"Florida!" Megan spat out with an attitude, as they all shook their heads no.

"Hmm . . . That brings us to the second question," said Miguel. "When New Yorkers talk about the tristate area, what states are included?" Miguel immediately pointed to the right side of the room, where most hands went up.

"New York, Connecticut, and New Jersey," said a voice I easily recognized. Oh, cool! It was Eliza's.

"Let me guess, is that the local section over there?" Jackie asked.

"Yes." Eliza laughed and joined us.

Miguel pointed at me. "You should be sitting over there with them!"

Lily and the girls gave me another weird stare. *What's up with them?*

"Let's get some of your girls from Florida to engage in a friendly competition," Jackie adds fuel to the fire. "Local girls versus out-of-towners!" Despite the weirdness, I was super proud that in this room of about one hundred dancers, my past and present friends were up here together. It felt amazing.

Miguel chose Megan and Trina and started the music. *This should be interesting.*

After a few minutes, Eliza and I were cheering our victory. The crowd had chosen us as the champs! And we'd scored apple key chains as parting gifts. Not bad for one class. Also, maybe a good souvenir gift for Hailey for her backpack. At the end, everyone gave our instructors a huge round of applause to show our appreciation.

"That was so fun!" said Eliza after I hugged her good-bye.

Isabella came from nowhere to stop and stare at me and Eliza. This class was so huge, she'd been here the entire time and we hadn't noticed. No sooner had Eliza walked away than Isabella intercepted me halfway to the Squad. "Aww, you two—super sweet," Isabella cooed and pursed her lips into a pout. "Harper, congrats on your acceptance into a Connecticut studio! The DanceStarz didn't deserve you."

I stared blankly at Isabella, though I had her all figured out.

"You know I'm still with DanceStarz," I said finally.

"Oh, really? It didn't seem like it," she said and continued down her own path.

When I chatted with the Squad, their mood was less jubilant. Apparently, they'd overheard my whole exchange with Isabella.

"Um, wasn't that amazing?" I asked the Squad. "Didn't you just love it?"

"It was the best," said Riley, cheerily. "Up until the part when you jumped ship and joined the competition."

"Hey, that was only for fun!" I chuckled, even though I wasn't entirely sure she was joking or not. I looked at everyone's faces for clues. They all looked happy, but also like they kind of thought what Riley had said was true. Why wouldn't they lighten up? Did they want me to change who I was? I was proud to be close to home, with my old friends. I knew that I could have friends in both worlds—but did they?

12

The walk back to our hotel was way more low-key than it had been when we were heading out to the surprise hip-hop class. We walked back across Times Square with way less enthusiasm than when we first saw it as a group. The flashing lights and all the flair might as well be dulled out by a dense gray fog. Even Riley kept her camera phone in her pocket most of the way—apart from the time she thought she saw Trey Thompson. (Spoiler: It wasn't him.)

"Well, that was kind of . . . funny," said Megan's mom to no one in particular. "Seeing Harper competing against her Squad members like that."

Megan pursed up her lips and puffed out a sigh.

"Nothing like a little fun competition to shake things up before our big day tomorrow," said Vanessa cheerfully. "Besides, it didn't mean anything. They were learning something new and having fun."

You would never catch Vanessa saying anything negative about competition and today was no different. She was the type of person who relished any opportunity to perform or watch a performance, in whatever form they came in.

Megan's mom wasn't going to let this go. "The day before nationals, I'd prefer more team bonding than in-team rivalry, but I guess that's just my preference. After all, team bonding is half the battle."

I knew this was just a dig at my hip-hop fun, and it wasn't fair. Here was the same woman whose daughter had thought nothing of acting like a rival to her teammates at regionals.

"Mom," said Megan, apparently issuing her mother a hint to cool it.

Wow. I hadn't seen that coming.

Even though I hadn't done it out loud, I instantly felt bad about dragging Megan like that. I had to admit, she'd been supportive and cool since regionals, and that went a long way.

I knew the Connecticut name drop was a fail, but I had been so swept up in the moment. It was like I'd forgotten that the portion of my life involving moving out of Connecticut and starting up a new school and a new dance studio had even happened. The same thing happened when I got sucked into the world of a good book or a cool movie. I'd get a little lost in it, and when I'd come out, it'd take half a second for the details of my real life to come rushing back in.

I was in New York, trying to help my new squad to victory, but that didn't mean I should feel bad hanging with my old friend.

And sorry, but today was super fun!

Megan and her mom—and whoever else had a problem with it—would just have to accept that.

That night in our hotel room, Lily and I started prepping for the next day. I definitely didn't want to forget anything! Lily started gathering up her things as I brushed my hair out postshower. Our favorite baking show was on in the background too.

"It's kind of ironic," said Lily as she packed her competition bag on her bed. "Today's dance-off between locals and out-of-towners kind of had a double meaning."

"Oh, really? How?" I asked.

I stopped brushing my hair, turned down the volume on the hotel TV a bit, and plopped down on my bed.

"Well, you could read that as your old life in Connecticut competing with your new one in Florida."

"Okay." I thought about it. "When you describe it that way, I guess I can see what you mean."

In the silence that followed, I picked up my brush and started plucking the hair strands from it.

"I guess if I'm honest, a part of me is being tugged in a different direction. It's been hard, since I want to hang with Eliza but do fun things with you guys too."

"I can see that," said Lily, refolding her hand towel to better fit in her bag. "Like when Eliza's around, I feel like you would rather hang with her than us."

Ouch.

"I don't do that," I said. Do I?

"Well, you may not think so, but that's how it looks from here."

I let out a slow sigh as what Lily had said sank in. I realized this was coming from my best friend on the Squad, and not from Megan, who did things just to rile people up. Or even from Riley, who could be a little extra. Lily had never told me anything to rile me up or cause drama. She did things that brought us closer. For once since we'd first met, it felt like she and I had slipped a little further apart these past few days.

It had happened right under my nose, and I hadn't even noticed until now. It was an issue that needed and, of course, deserved my attention. But right now was not the time. My brain was on overload. I was exhausted. We only had room to focus on one thing right now, and that was tomorrow's group competition.

"Lily," I said. "Can we talk about this later?"

"Sure." She sighed. "Later."

"e got this! Go big or go home!" Megan barked, her voice bouncing off the rows of closed hotel room doors.

She was not wrong.

Today was day one of the competition. If we didn't make it past this first round of group performances, that would be the end of the line for the Squad's chances at nationals.

But we were hours away from our performance. We were on our way to breakfast.

"Whoa, Megan," said Lily. "That's a lot of pep talk for someone just hoping to get their key card working again."

"In Riley's defense, those key cards are super touchy sometimes," said Trina. "The struggle is real."

Riley ignored us and kept trying to get the light on the door's safety lock to stop flashing red. She'd waved her key card this way and that. It was tough to watch.

"You seem to have everything you need," I gently told her. "You sure you have to go back in right now?"

Riley didn't turn around, which made her voice sound even more panicky. "But I need it! It's my lucky ring!"

"I thought you said you got it from a gumball machine," said Megan, totally unsympathetic. We could almost hear a record scratch when Megan's words flew out of her mouth.

Poor Riley. It didn't take a genius to figure out that this freak-out moment was not just about a lucky ring. This was about the competition today. I was used to competing. We all were. But for me, competition days usually played out the same way. I got quiet and focused, I usually worked off my nerves by feeding my team with extra encouragement, hoping some of that pep talk would also indirectly boost my own confidence. Lily zoned out to her music. And after competing with the Squad, I'd come to recognize how they take on preperformance jitters.

Right then, just as I thought we'd be there forever, we

finally heard a soft *click*, and Riley opened her door. She was out of her room before you know it, and sporting a tiny heart ring around her right pinkie.

At last, we could meet Vanessa and the moms down the hall at the elevators. There was a cushioned bench right by the elevators they enjoyed sitting on to chat and strategize as they waited on us to be ready. To our surprise, they were still standing when we got there.

I guessed we weren't the only ones managing our worries about today.

"Eat something," Riley's mom told us a few minutes later as we wordlessly pushed food around our plates but did not eat much.

Riley sat back in her seat, one hand laying a fork down flat and spinning it against the table. "I'll be fine. I'm just not that hungry."

"Well, you girls have to eat something if you want to perform with any oomph," said Megan's mom.

This was getting hopeless. All of our positive vibes were draining from us, and I couldn't let that happen. I leaned forward in my seat and made eye contact with each girl.

"The best fuel we could use right now is our Squad cheer. Who's with me?" I ask, a little louder and punchier than expected. I guess it's true that we have to fake it till we make it.

"Let's do it," said Trina. She nudged Riley next to her.

"Fine, it couldn't hurt," said Megan, whose response surprised everyone.

"Lily?" I said in a small voice, nervous that my good friend was still being kind of weird. After she'd brought up how she felt I was trying to pick Eliza over the Squad, we had left things at that and gone to bed. We wanted to get ready early and gather everything we couldn't pack the night before, so there wasn't more discussion this morning, either. Okay, maybe we had time but we didn't want to face it.

At least I didn't. But now I had some regrets about that decision.

Lily looked down at her plate, picking at her food, ignoring me, and all of our stares.

"She's ignoring us," Megan said. "Who made Lily so mad she's not speaking to us? I've never seen her like this before."

Huh? This is bad. Super bad.

"Lily?" Trina reached across the table and touched Lily's hand.

"Wha—?" Startled, Lily almost jumped out of her chair. She reached under her curtain of long hair and pulled out her earbuds.

"Did you say something?"

We all cracked up. It was like unleashing a flood of relief, jitters, resentment, and annoyance all at once. The more we laughed in a chorus of wacky, loud, and quiet snickering, the more contagious the laughter became. Riley was cracking up so hard, she was tapping on the table and gasping for air.

"What happened to those pink headphones you're always wearing?" I asked her.

"I didn't have room in my bag, so I switched things up," said Lily, still confused by what all the fuss was but laughing anyway.

"Well, guess there's no need for that team cheer anymore," said Riley. "I think I got the emergency mood transplant I needed."

With that, she picked up her fork and dug into her eggs and fruit salad. And a bagel with cream cheese and her first-ever lox.

"Yum," she said, grinning.

There were throngs of people making their way to the performance ballroom. I thought it had been as crowded the last time, but day-before-showtime crowded is another thing entirely than hour-before-showtime.

We all stuck close together. When we finally got off the elevator, we tried to beat the crowd for the sign-in desk. Vanessa said something to Lily, who turned to me to repeat it.

"Psst . . . She's about to pass out the credentials," said Lily.

"Somebody passed out? Who passed out?" Riley's mom had already reached into her large handbag and pulled out her first aid kit.

"No one," I reassured her. "Everyone is fine. Vanessa is just about to give us our performer IDs we need to flash as we come in and out of the dressing rooms."

As soon as we wear the passes around our necks, we're allowed to veer away from the slow-moving crowd of vendors, yet-to-be registered performers, their families, and early bird audience members and gain access to the equivalent of a backstage pass.

"Whew, there's room to breathe back here," said Riley when we stepped into the spacious room—or "chill zone," as Trina started calling it—we were to share with other performers. Several dance groups were already here, doing warm-up stretches or just lounging around. One section was partitioned and repurposed as private changing rooms. The carpeted floors gave it a cozy but elegant vibe, and people felt comfortable enough to sit on the floor. We could hear the music from the grand ballroom from here, but it was muffled down to a distant hum.

Lily gasped. "There's one last free corner!" We couldn't believe our luck. As fast as our legs could carry us—the speed walk was something we learned to do since arriving here—we claimed that corner by dropping all our bags.

With help from the moms, we began doing our makeup and hair. Whichever one of us was free would head to the neighboring room to run through a super-low-impact version of the dance. Vanessa's last-minute feedback went a long way in preparing us and encouraging us to dig deeper.

On my way back to rejoin the Squad, my name rang out as soon as I stepped foot into the chill zone.

"Harper!"

I turned to the source of my shout-out and instantly cracked a smile when I saw who it was.

"Eliza!"

Wow, who would imagine the both of us—Eliza and Harper—together on the big stage? We even got a chance to dance together at the hip-hop class yesterday. But today was a day we'd both talked endlessly about: the chance to compete at an event as huge and respected as nationals. Here we were. Rival dance troupes but still teamed up in a lot of ways. I was rooting for her, and I was sure she was rooting for me.

We gave each other a double fist bump and then a high five in greeting, already in game day mode. Much like a basketball player at the free-throw line, Eliza had a focused look in her eyes. Her hands were at her hips, and her stance was wide and stabling. Her track suit jacket was half zipped, so her navy-blue, sparkly performance bodysuit stayed visible. She looked like a temporarily benched player, ready to jump in at the first whistle.

"Ready to start off strong?" she asked.

"Always." I looked her square in the eyes. "We all are. You?"

She nodded sharply. "All day."

"I know it. You were born for this."

"You were too, girlie." Eliza gave me another high five. "Let's show them what we're all about."

"Good luck to you and Dance City!"

"Good luck to you and DanceStarz!"

Members of Eliza's squad had been too busy sprucing up or warming up to notice or care about our chat. But when I turned around and headed back to my camp, it was an entirely different story. Busted, my Squad sprang into action, doing stretches, texting like normal, as if they hadn't been doing anything else but staring and trying to lip-read my short conversation with Eliza.

"So," said Megan a snarky tone. "Did she talk to you about the routines she'll do?"

"What? No, of course not. I would never ask her that." I frowned at her.

"Oh," she continued, pretending to be confused by my defensiveness. "Well, did you tell her anything about what we'll be doing?"

Okay, now I was really annoyed.

"Who would even do that? You and I must not have met before." I rolled my eyes, offended.

Looking around, I didn't see Lily, or Trina, or even Riley making a move to intervene. "You guys don't think I would do that, do you?"

"Of course not," Lily said. "But . . ."

But? But what?

Megan's voice rose inches higher than your average speaking decibel. "Well, maybe we just know the Florida Harper and not the Connecticut one all that well."

"What's that supposed to mean?" I asked, both mad and upset.

"It means you're different here," Lily said, her eyes looking down.

"I'm the same me I always was!" I protested. "I mean, I'm

the old me, which is still the new me! I mean—"

Our squabble drew the attention of a few performers in the closest spot next to us. Thankfully, the performances had begun, and aside from the music, the din of the crowd and the announcer's voice filled the air with buffering sound.

Megan's mom set down her sparkle eyeshadow case, paused from doing Trina's makeup, and walked over. "Okay, girls, there's no need bickering about this now. Harper is allowed to say hello to a friend—even if it's a rival performer right before you're about to dance at highest level this Squad has ever competed on."

Thanks, I think?

"Now you two should remind yourself that you'll be sharing a stage soon, so you better start acting like the teammates I know you are."

At least she didn't force us to apologize to one another, as if we were toddlers. I retreated to the farthest corner from everyone and threw on my earbuds. My plan was to zone everyone and everything out—Megan's wrath, Lily's disappointment, Trina's sympathy, Riley's judgment, Eliza's expectations. For the next half hour, it was just me and the music on my favorite playlist.

Someone tapped my foot, and my eyes flew open.

"Harper," said Riley's mom. "They've given the fifteen-minute warning. Let's head to the stage."

The girls were already out of their track suits and rocking their shiny silver-with-crochet-trim bodysuits. I stepped out of my track suit fast and walked with the group to the real backstage.

It was showtime.

It was just us and Vanessa backstage. Finally. The moms had gone to their designated seats in the audience to watch and film our performance.

The roar of the crowd sounded arena-size. We listened off-stage, absorbing all the pumped-up energy that came with it.

This was nationals.

We were here. This was what I needed to focus on.

After speaking to the woman with the clipboard, Vanessa turned to us. We huddled around her and hung on to her every word.

"Okay, girls, this is the moment you've been training so hard for. You belong here. And for the next five minutes, that stage out there is all yours. So just have fun and let your talent and love for dance shine, inside and out."

At the end of her talk, I noticed for the first time that we were all holding hands. Trina was on my right, Riley was to my left, and directly across was Megan. She and I caught each other's eyes and held them for a moment, connecting in a more peaceful way than the scene ten minutes ago.

Had Vanessa witnessed that, she would have been livid. I thought of her special request that we conduct ourselves as professionals. I hoped to make that up with a flawless routine now.

"DanceStarz on three!" I called out with my hand in the center of the huddle, palm faced down.

Lily was the first to stack her hand on top of mine. We looked at each other and smiled. Megan was next, followed by Riley, Trina, and Vanessa.

"DanceStarz!" we all shouted.

The group onstage ended their routine in a pyramid pose—which was tricky to hold for as long as they were currently doing. They waited for the applause to pick up before coming out of the pose to wave at the crowd. They exited to the opposite end of the stage.

The MC jumped into action, excited. His words reverberated throughout the ballroom. "Let them hear how much you enjoyed that!"

Riley made a strange sound that was a mix of a gasp and one of her cat's furballs getting stuck in her throat.

Vanessa went into EMT mode. "You need water? Are you okay?"

I patted Riley's back. The rest of the girls looked at each other in panic. Oh, no. This was not a good time for an emergency. But Riley nodded and shooed us back to give her some room.

"The MC," she said between breaths, her hand on her chest. "I recognize his voice. It's . . . it's Trey Thompson!"

I shook my head. "Seriously, Riley?"

"It is?" Trina asked, intrigued. She tiptoed near the stage curtain to steal a peek at him. Then she looked back at us and nodded. Whoa!

"I WAS RIGHT!" Riley said, beaming. "My Trey-dar was going off!"

"Riley, you scared us half to death," Vanessa quietly scolded her. "Now, I don't know who this Trey Thompson is, but I'm sure he's not worth your distraction right now."

"TREY THOMPSON is worth everything!" Riley shouted. Then she caught herself. "Yes, Vanessa."

As we waited for the MC—that is, the one and only Trey— to announce us, I subconsciously started jumping in place, Jackie and Miguel style. It was surprisingly a good way to stay pumped yet focused, and work off the false alarm about Riley.

Riley joined in, because she no doubt needed to do the same. Trina, Lily, and Megan also joined in, and then pretty soon we all were doing the Jackie and Miguel. Vanessa included!

"All the way from Florida, please welcome, from Dance-Starz Academy, central Florida regional champs . . . the Squad!"

WOO HOO!!! THAT'S US!!!!

"Watch your feet," Trina whispered.

"Be high energy," Riley said.

We all gathered around in a tight circle to do the ritual we'd made up as a squad.

"Dance!" Trina led the cheer.

Lily, Megan, Trina, Riley, and I all did a little dance move.

"Starz!" Trina continued.

We fluttered our fingers like sparkling stars. Then we leaned into a huddle and said:

"Squad!"

I guess we were riding on the coattails of the group we followed, because the applause was still going and more energized than I'd expected. But it only served to pump us up even more!

In a straight line, we strutted out, spotlighting with our profiles to the huge audience. We proceeded, each with one arm extended and held straight in the air above our heads, keeping our index fingers pointed to the sky. Our other hands rested steadily on our hips, our elbows pointed outward. Step left, step right, step left, step right.

The illuminated stage backdrop came into full view. It was a beast—larger than life. It was possibly three stories high or more. The image spread across the massive stage was a sophisticated illustration of New York's world famous buildings. Above that was the official event logo, followed by—in fancy lettering—

WELCOME TO THE 44TH ANNUAL NATIONALS!

Awesome! Vanessa couldn't have dreamed this up better herself. The backdrop was perfect for our dance, and we hadn't even planned on it! So lucky!

Because our new dance theme was: NEW YORK, NEW YORK!

When we reached center stage, one arm still in the air and the other still on our hips, we pivoted in sync and faced forward. I caught a glimpse of the size of the crowd. Whoa! I didn't know if I had ever been in front of such a huge audience! EEP! Thankfully, I immediately recovered from my surprise and flashed a broad smile. There were stage lights in our eyes, but the sea of people seemed to go beyond the horizon line.

The crowd cheered out of sheer curiosity. That's when we lifted our other arms into the air too, and began to join all our sky-high hands to form differently shaped peaks. In each peak, the taller person kept their finger pointing up. When it registered with the audience that we in our shimmering slate-silver bodysuits and tall arm peaks were New York's skyscrapers, they roared with applause. We held the pose until the bass dropped and started thumping.

The music mix was filled with city sound effects that weren't overpowering but were just so catchy when woven together the way they were. Horns blaring, people shouting, trains screeching—all to a steady beat you wanted to get up and dance to. In fact, a part of the crowd could be heard clapping along.

We took long, rhythmic strides past, between, behind, and in front of each other, like we were trying to tie the air into a big messy knot. Then we broke away, each of us bursting into different styles of dance, mimicking what happens every day on New York's sidewalks. Riley leapt in the air, one arm high, as if hailing a cab. Megan swayed side to side to the music, as if trying to keep her balance on a fast-moving subway. Lily, Trina, and I made like we were holding an animated conversation on the street. Our backs arching, heads bobbing, arms flailing with every change in tempo. Riley was especially on fire. She must have been working extra hard for that first-place photo op with Trey Thompson. Hey, whatever motivated her.

Finally, we all gathered in a line across the stage and pretended to turn and jump in a giant double Dutch rope, our moves alternated between windmill arms for the turners and the acrobatics and fancy footwork of the jumpers inside the imaginary two egg-beater ropes.

There must've been a large local crowd here, because they sounded like they recognized so much in our movements and were celebrating every city slicker we had met so far!

Vanessa really knew what she was doing with this choreo!

As the music wound down, we went back into our frenzied city walking we did earlier in the dance. We added extra-special drama with leaps and one nonstop, warp-speed spin, performed by—ahem, ME! The music evolved into jazzy sounds that played out in cool chaos. The horns went all high-pitched and whiny, while the piano keys sounded as if a cat was walking across them. And then, slowly and steadily, we became one giant knot, bunched up and tugging, grabbing hold of each other's hands. As the strings took over, we kept our hands together, but untied ourselves into one straight line across the stage. We lifted our arms into the air, the peaks once again on display. We had become the New York skyline once more.

The crowd was on their feet, whooping and shouting their love for our routine.

YES! A clean routine!

We lowered our arms and took a slow, grateful bow. Overwhelmingly happy with the crowd reception, we bowed a second time. Well, all of us, that is, except Riley—who froze in place when she saw Trey Thompson make his way back to the stage.

"Representing DanceStarz Academy in Florida, ladies and gentlemen, the Squad!"

As the crowd cheered, Trey turned around and looked at us.

"From Florida, really? Don't they look about ready to enroll in *NYC High*?" he asked the crowd.

"YES!" Riley couldn't help herself around Trey Thompson, and she shout-answered him.

The crowd raucously applauded their agreement.

We trotted offstage feeling light and airy. My most pressing issue was I wanted to burst into wild, messy cheers, but I had to keep my composure as I exited the stage. It felt like holding my breath underwater. When we were finally out of sight from the audience, we screamed! We jumped into Vanessa's waiting arms for a group hug! Yes, Vanessa was pumped up too!

But this group seemed a little small. Wait a minute—

"Where's Riley?" I asked.

We didn't see her anywhere.

"OMG, look!" shouted Lily, who pointed back to the stage, where Riley stood alone and in a daze, staring at the back of Trey Thompson's head.

"Somebody should go get her," Megan said. She touched her nose. "NOT IT."

Trina and Lily touched their noses in a *not it* signal. Okay, I was IT. I got to be embarrassed. Fine. I spun onto the stage as if this were part of the performance. When I got to Riley, I took her hand and spun her around once, before I walked her off—pretty much dragged her off—with our arms linked.

"Let's go, city girl," I said. "You'll have plenty of opportunity to see dream boy at *NYC High*."

The rest of our hours in the chill room were just that—chill. We were proud of our performance, so we had no trouble eating lunch when it was brought in for everyone.

"Maybe we should grab an extra bottle of water," I said. "In case Riley here chokes on a furball again." Everyone cracked up, teasing Riley about all her drama.

"Good thinking," said Trina.

"This time we'll have to keep a close eye on her." Megan rolled her eyes, but in a joking way.

"How'd it go?" Eliza asked me as she passed me by on her way to her lunch line.

"I think okay?" I said. She gave me a thumbs-up and said, "Same."

It seemed there were strong performances by many, if not all of the teams who returned to the chill room, relieved and congratulating one another. I hated to admit it, but Megan's mom was right. This was a level of competition we were not used to. There were no amateurs here. We weren't the only ones who'd had a good day. Now came the tough part—finding out if it was our last day here. If we didn't place high enough, we were out.

EEK.

"No matter what the results are out there, you should be so proud of yourselves. You owned that stage today," said Vanessa before she led us to the designated area in front of the stage for all contestants.

Arriving at the grand ballroom on floor level gave us a different view of the crowd, the stage and its huge skyline backdrop, and, of course, the MC himself.

"There he is!" Riley grabbed Megan's arm. "TREY!"

"Pull yourself together, girl," Megan said. "He's a human being like the rest of us."

Mesmerized by Trey Thompson, Riley was back to her antics. She cleared her throat. Loudly. And then she tripped over her feet because she wasn't looking at where she was going. We all just shook our heads and guided her for her own sake. We were shuffled to the middle of the pack, but we had decent sightlines.

"Ladies and gentleman, was that an amazing morning of excellent performances or what?" Trey hyped up the crowd.

"Yeaahhhhh!" One cheerer was way louder than everyone else. I grinned at Riley. I actually appreciated her enthusiasm for Trey—it was cracking me up and taking the edge off my nerves.

"Performers, you hear that applause? That's every one of us in this place saying that you all are winners." The applause grew in intensity as Trey pumped his fist. "Let them hear it, yes?"

"Aw, thanks, Trey!"" Riley called out, as if they were the only two people in the room.

"Without further ado, we have the envelope with the judges' tallies and the three top-scoring teams who will return tomorrow for the final round of group competition."

The mood changed. There were audible gasps as all the dancers got serious. This was it.

We all held one another's hands and sat closer together.

"Our first nationals results," Megan whispered fiercely.

"From Trey Thompson." Riley sighed happily. Megan shot her a look that definitely tried to put her priorities straight. The top ten teams were announced. We were not numbered ten through four. So that meant we'd either placed or were completely shut out. And gone. And sent away. *Okay, Harper, pull yourself together,* I told myself.

"In third place, hailing all the way from Arizona, the Scottsdale Steppers!"

The group leapt up from their spot and didn't stop jumping until the trophy was in their arms. It was such a display of pure emotion, you couldn't help but smile and feel happy for them. They accepted their day one qualifying medals and posed for a photo with Trey.

"I almost started jumping up and down with them!" he said. That guy was all in. I was starting to appreciate him. Not as much as Riley did, though.

Two more slots to go.

"Let's keep this celebrations going, shall we?" He flashed a dimpled smile, which of course was followed by low-key swooning. "In second place, representing Florida . . ."

"Florida!" Trina burst out. "We're from Florida! Is anyone else from Florida?"

We gripped each other's hands and practically bit our tongues not to cheer prematurely, just in case those medals were meant for another lucky team from Florida that we didn't know existed.

". . . the Squad, of DanceStarz Academy!"

AHHHHHHH!!!

We placed! At NATIONALS! I could see Vanessa and the moms standing up and cheering for us wildly.

We all jumped up and went to get our trophy. The crowd cheered with so much gusto, we felt the need to wave our thanks to them when we got onstage.

Megan held her hands out to take the trophy, but Riley basically tripped her to get to Trey first.

"The pull of Trey is too strong," I whispered to Lily, who giggled as Riley grasped the trophy but didn't take it out of Trey's hands, trying to prolong the moment. I think he was used to dealing with fans.

"Your performance was one of my faves," he said with such honesty.

"Thank you," said Riley, all heart-eyes. "Thank you, Trey Thompson."

When we posed for a photo with him, you don't have to guess who stood right next to Trey.

"And you guys made fun of me for saying I would meet Trey!" Riley suddenly turned on us.

"They did?" Trey said. "Well, let this be a lesson that dreams can come true."

"You're right, Riley," I said seriously. "We were wrong."

"Also, we should probably announce the winners," Trey said gently. *Oops!*

We grinned and said cheese and floated off the stage in a state of euphoria. Dragging Riley with us. As we sat down onstage, I realized there was one name I had yet to hear. I hoped I would hear it now, for first place.

"And now, our top spot," Trey announced. He paused, dragging out the suspense. "Come on up, Dance City of Connecticut, and get your first-place qualifier medals and trophy!"

Wow. Eliza and the team actually did it.

"Whooo!" I shouted, clapping for my good friend. Her team had come with their A-game and nabbed the top prize. I was impressed.

If only my teammates were half as impressed. They clapped politely. Megan looked pointedly at me cheering loudly for Eliza.

"The competition is not over," Megan muttered. "We still have the chance to knock Dance City out the top spot and be the overall winner tomorrow."

I just ignored Megan and kept on clapping, But I did agree with her that it wasn't over. We'd gone big, so we were not going home . . . yet.

After the competition, Vanessa had another surprise in store.

"Girls, I have a treat for you," Vanessa said. "This is not only a reward for all of your hard work, but it's inspiration and motivation."

"I wonder what this could be," I said. "Maybe we are going to see *Hamilton*? Or *Dear Evan Hansen*?"

Lily laughed. "I wish! Those tickets are super hard to get right now!"

"Hey, we can dream!" I said.

We walked for a bit until we saw the famous sign: RADIO CITY MUSIC HALL.

"Ooooh, are we going to see the Rockettes?" I yell. We all start cheering.

The Rockettes is one of the most famous dance companies

in the world. Just seeing Radio City Music Hall was an inspiration.

Vanessa laughed. "Even better. You are going to dance with them!"

We all stood there, stunned. Then we burst into more cheers. *Dance? With the Rockettes? What?!*

I was so excited!!

"Have you ever done this before?" Lily asked. I shook my head no. This was going to be AWESOME!

We were greeted by one of the tour people, who welcomed us and showed us around a little bit.

"Hi, everyone! I'm Matt." He gave us a cheerful wave.

"I want to give you a little history of the company before you go on to do this dance experience," he explained. "So the Rockettes are a precision dance company that has been performing since 1933 with their most famous show, the Radio City Christmas Spectacular."

We learned that the building was designed in the art deco style in the early 1930s. Its biggest room was a huge auditorium, and they included red seats because the people who built the theater thought that would make it successful. It was beautiful! We looked around at the deep reds and golds, and it did look very luxurious.

Then, suddenly, a voice called out from the back of the room.

"Vanessa!"

A tall woman wearing a black leotard and leggings and high heels with her hair in a tight ponytail came running up to Vanessa. The two of them hugged, and that's when I saw what was written on the woman's tank top:

THE RADIO CITY ROCKETTES

"Vanessa knows a Rockette?" Megan whispered.

"Yes, she does." The Rockette had overheard her and smiled. "My name is Jen. Vanessa and I went to dance camp together. She knows it was always my dream to become a Rockette!"

"I'm so proud she accomplished her dream," Vanessa said. "Jen, I'd like to introduce you to the elite dance team of Dance-Starz Academy of Florida."

We were all really excited to meet her and then even more excited once she said she was going to lead our experience.

"So let me tell you a little bit about the Rockettes!" Jen said. "The dance company has been around for almost a century. More than one million people see us dance every year. There are main dancers and swings who can fill in the spots if needed."

"The very first choreographer founded the American chorus line," she continued. "We are most known for that dance line, where we do our eye-high kicks."

"And your glittery costumes that you wear!" Riley piped in. "One of my dreams is to be a costume designer—maybe I could be for the Rockettes!"

"Riley is our resident fashion-designer-to-be," Vanessa said, which surprised us all and made Riley glow to be called out in front of one of her heroes.

Jen nodded. "I have no doubt you would be great at designing! Many of our costumes are glamorous. But we do have one that's a little different. For those who aren't as familiar with the show, we have a big routine where we have wooden soldier costumes, with big hats and giant pants." We all smiled.

"That's the dance with the soldiers falling on each other like dominoes," I whisper to Lily.

"If any of you like to do hair and makeup, I'll point out that we have to do our own hair—usually I do a French twist—and our own makeup before every show! We do have a wardrobe assistant to help us with our costume changes," Jen continued.

"The choreography includes several kinds of dance, so we have to be proficient in tap, jazz and ballet. It's a challenge to have every count perfect.

"One of the challenges some dancers face is that you have to be part of a line, so you don't have the opportunity to be a soloist," Jen said.

I peeked up at Megan to see if she'd caught that.

"Every year, about five hundred people audition. It's hard work, as we rehearse six hours a day, six days a week, for approximately six weeks before we start the show. Every show has three hundred kicks in it! And we do up to four shows in one day! Every move we make is detailed, including how high we hold our arms and how high we kick and where our eyes are looking."

"Whoa!" Trina said, and we all laughed.

Jen clapped her hands. "So! Are you girls ready to learn some Rockettes dancing with me?"

Yes! Jen took us into a room that look like one of our practice rooms. Just like our own rehearsals, we started with warm-ups and stretches. She had us all pull our hair off our faces, into tight, high ponytails.

Then we started with strut kicks. Jen had us all get in a line facing forward. She counted off:

"One, two, three, four, and on five put your right hand straight up in the air! On seven, put your arms around each other. Step left and kick! Step ball change and passé!"

I got to stand next to Jen in the line, which was both awesome and kind of nerve-wracking! We all had our arms around one another—although Jen told us not to really touch one another but barely touch the fabric on our tops—and we were kicking straight out but not as high as the Rockettes would kick. I looked at Lily next to me, and we grinned. Then I looked the other direction, and I could hardly believe I had my arm around a real Rockette and was dancing with her in a kick line!

Then we moved to the most famous move they did: the eye-high kicks! "Five, six, seven, eight—"

Quick jump and then right kick! Left! Right! Left! Double left!

I tried to keep my leg straight and kick super high. Megan was pretty well known for her leg holds in high kicks, so she definitely nailed this part.

"Megan is very flexible," Jen said approvingly.

We managed to learn a whole mini routine.

"I love the bubbly energy of the girl on the end!" Jen said, pointing at Lily. "Enthusiasm and personality are important traits. Keep that energy high!"

We went through the routine a few more times. It was so fun!

"When you're known for being a precision dance group, precise footwork certainly is critical." Jen nodded at Trina approvingly. "Your footwork is excellent."

Then I got my chance to shine.

"You," she said. "You hold your head incredibly still, which is an underrated skill. Did you know that?"

"Um, kind of," I said. "I practice spotting for my turn series, which are my favorite."

"Oh, I'd love to see your turn series," she said.

Okay! I took my prep and held my plié for a second. Then I pulled up spotting six consecutive turns and landed gracefully.

"Beautiful!" Jen clapped for me. *Yay!* Then I got back in line with the other girls.

"Do you have any questions for me?" Jen asked.

I raised my hand.

"What did it feel like when you auditioned and then they called your name and said that you'd made it?" I asked.

"It was the best feeling in the world!" Jen's face lit up. "I'd worked so hard and wanted it for so long. When they said my name, I screamed. Then I alternated crying with joy and laughing for about two days."

We all laughed.

"Along with dancing the Spectacular, what's your favorite part?" Lily asked.

"Performing in the Macy's Thanksgiving Day Parade!" Jen said. "Have any of you ever performed in a parade?"

At that, everybody turned to look at me. Because the first time I'd performed in a parade with the Squad, I had—ugh, it was still so embarrassing to say—fallen off the float. I couldn't help but groan.

"Oh dear, I may have hit a nerve!" Jen read the room.

"My last parade wasn't the best, but I'm over it." I laughed.

"She got on TV!" Trina pointed out kindly. "Not falling, I mean. Dancing."

"Being on TV is another fun bonus of being a Rockette," Jen said. "We perform on shows a lot. Oh, hello!"

Five more dancers walked in the room, also wearing the leotards and character shoes with high heels.

"We hear there's an amazing dance team here for nationals," one of the girls said.

She meant us!

"Do you mind if we join you?" one of them asked. "Would you like to dance the routine Jen taught you with us?"

Mind? We all scrambled excitedly into place.

"Five, six, seven, eight!"

And we danced! Kick! Ball change! I felt like I was a real Rockette! And when I did my strut kicks, I swear I even looked like one!

When it was over, we all started clapping. This was probably the best thing EVER. And we had fun as a group. No fighting, no drama, no weird things about Eliza. It finally felt like we were enjoying ourselves, both onstage and off. I hoped this feeling would keep on going.

14

After our amazing Rockettes experience, I had one more thing left to do—something I had been looking forward to for a while. It had all been cleared with Vanessa and my parents—I was going to Connecticut to visit my old dance school! People who lived outside New York City usually drove into Manhattan for dinner, not the other way around. Eliza's mom was willing to bet we'd be headed against traffic both ways.

I hoped she was right.

I was honestly starting to get a little tired. Our schedule had been really busy. And even though we really loved the cool experiences Vanessa set up for us, we had something planned every day outside of the competition. I loved that I was living out so many dreams. But it was both great and exhausting.

Suddenly, I missed Hailey, my parents, and my dog. I decided to video chat Hailey.

"Harper!" she answered—no, shrieked—into my cell phone screen. It was funny what a little distance could do for a sibling. Hailey was often my number one fan, but she seemed so much more excited when I called from far away.

"What are you all up to?" I was just as happy to see her. She was holding a mixing spoon and had one of the aprons that had come with the cooking show set she'd gotten for her birthday.

"Hello? We were all watching on live stream! We saw your competition!"

"Thank you!"

"You were like this!" She held her spoon up in a pose. "Then this!" Hailey dance-posed around the room with her bowl and spoon and then went offscreen.

"Uh, Hailey," I said. "I can't see you."

"Oh!" She popped back onscreen. She showed me the goopy brown contents of her bowl. "Anyway, I'm making you celebration brownies."

"Thanks? But I'm not even there," I said. "You know I'm not going to be back for a few days?"

"Hee-hee," she said. "I know. But that's what I told Mom so she'd let me bake. Sorry you'll miss them."

"Let me speak to Mo." I shook my head when I imagined the mess she was creating.

"Mo, it's Harper! Come on and say hi." Hailey pointed the camera to Mo, who was clearly searching the kitchen for me.

"Not there, Mo." I cracked up. "I'm over here."

"He's all confused." Hailey laughed.

Just then, a text came through. It had to be Eliza.

We're downstairs.

"Oh, I gotta go, Hailey. Eliza's here."

"Are you going to Connecticut?" Hailey screamed. "Don't forget to say hi to Timothy the squirrel!"

"Um, I'll try. And tell Mom and Dad I said hi," I said. "Give Mo squishes for me."

I hung up and zipped around the hotel room to grab my bag and my shoes. *What else, what else?* My key card! My phone was in my hand, but I kept feeling like there was something else I was forgetting. I hated when I got that nagging feeling, but couldn't figure it out. Oh, well. It would come to me. I headed out the door and across the hall. After a few knocks, Vanessa came out to escort me down.

"Ready to be reunited with your old crew?" She smiled.

"I'm ready for it all. Being in Connecticut again is going to be bananas." I was sure I had the same dreamy look Riley had had when looking at Trey.

"Well, have a wonderful time, and we'll see you back here later tonight." Vanessa waved to Eliza's mom, who was right outside the elevator doors.

"Thanks, Vanessa!" I said before hugging Eliza hello with a squeal. Eliza sat up front with her mom, and I sat in the back seat, looking out the window. I recognized some of the sites we passed as Eliza's mom drove us out of the city, although mostly I had taken the train when I'd lived here.

"Look!" I pointed at the sign that said WELCOME TO CONNECTICUT.

Eliza filled me in on all the gossip from the dance studio. I wished I had more time to visit with my old school friends too, but I just didn't have enough before we both had to get back.

However, Eliza's mom had a little surprise for me on the way to the dance studio. She pulled off an exit early, and right away I knew where we were going.

"I thought you'd like to swing by for a moment," Eliza's mom said kindly.

My old neighborhood! We drove up the street and passed my former neighbors' houses. When we got to my old house, Eliza's mom stopped the car.

It looked exactly the same. Except for some holiday decorations in the window that obviously were not ours. So the same. But different.

Our new house was so different from this one, which had three floors and not as many windows, and enormous trees that have lost their leaves surrounding it. I stared up at my old bedroom window and wondered if they had repainted my purple walls.

"I hate to interrupt, but we have to move forward," Eliza's mom said.

Yes, I had to move forward.

"Is that weird to look at your old house and know that it's not your house anymore?" Eliza asked. "That would kind of drive me crazy knowing that somebody else was living in my bedroom! And using my bathroom! Also, I would miss it so much—I don't know how you do it!"

I slumped down in my seat. I mean, it's not like I had a choice. I was mostly quiet as we turned a few corners and then pulled up into a familiar parking lot.

Dance City Studios!

My old studio! It looked exactly the same as it had when I'd left!

"Come on," said Eliza, leading me from the parking lot through the glass front door.

"Harper, is that you?" Lucinda, the receptionist, was at the front desk, looking just like I remembered her. "Have you come back to visit us?" She came around the desk for a big hug.

"We miss you around here, you know. The little ones have been asking where you went." She smiled.

That made me both happy and sad to hear, but I couldn't start bawling so soon into my visit. This was only the first minute. *Sniff.* Okay, maybe I could. I blinked back my tears. We moved on, passing by classes in session. Through the glass, I caught glimpses of each one. Wow, being here was making old memories come back to me. I remembered the time I'd spent to perfect my signature spin in the classroom we were walking by.

"She's here!" Eliza ran down the hallway and threw her arms around me. "We're having a party for you! Okay, not exactly for you."

Everyone was gathered there for a special Friday-Night-In fundraiser. Proceeds were to go toward raising tuition fees for one talented dancer of limited means. There was pizza, music, and dancing, so I was glad to be there. I'd missed New York–style pizza. So badly. It didn't matter that this was my second time eating pizza. I would eat it for breakfast, lunch, dinner, and dessert when I was here!

"Look who's here!" Eliza called out.

"HARPER!"

I got the coolest greeting ever imagined. Some of my old dance team, and only a few new ones I hadn't recognized. Some I'd gone to school with. A girl hugged me and more came over to say hi.

Some kids were classmates at my old middle school, others I knew just from the dance studio.

"Oh my gosh, when did you come back?" someone else asked.

"How's life in Florida?" my old neighbor Caty asked.

"It's cool, actually," I said.

"Don't you mean 'warm'?" she joked. Everyone groaned.

"Yeah, that is so weird," I said. "We wore shorts for Thanksgiving! It feels way more normal to be here in winter."

"Well, they can't be up on the latest dances like we are up here," another dancer commented. I recognized her as someone from the junior squad.

"In a way—they have their own style. It's different, but it's no less cool," I told them. "Dancing is huge there, too. We have great dancers."

"She's right! Her team was amazing yesterday!" Eliza said. Then she smiled mischievously. "I do have to point out that we did beat you."

"OOOOooooooh." Everyone laughed.

"Bring it," I shot back. "That was just practice. Also, I was the one who taught you how to do that turn, so your victory is partially mine."

Everyone laughed again. I cracked a smile, unsure if it was betraying my friends.

Then I laughed as hard as everyone else. But they were just kidding around. No need to take any offense.

One or two people were already dancing, teaching one another new dance moves and practicing with one another.

"This is such a good idea for a party," I told Eliza, looking around as I folded my slice of pepperoni. You know what else is a good idea? New York pizza."

"Yeah, this is something new we started about six months ago," she explained as she scooped extra cheese balls onto her plate. "It's already helping two students stay on here, when before they wouldn't have been able to."

"That's amazing," I said, touched by the story.

Kelly, a girl who had been in a few of my classes but I didn't know well, walked over and joined the conversation. She was one of the people who danced a lot with Eliza though.

"So, congrats on qualifying for round two! That's sooo great!" She congratulated me as though she were overacting. There was something weird about it, but I shrugged it off.

Beyond high-fiving each other, Eliza and I hadn't really spoken about what had happened, even about the fact that we were kind of in a fierce competition here. I wasn't about to examine why we didn't go there, but something was telling us to stay on safer topics. My neighbor was about to mess up that unspoken agreement between Eliza and me. So I changed the subject.

"So how crazy was it that Trey Thompson MCed the competition today?!" I said.

I was hoping someone in here had a Riley-level celebrity crush on him. Maybe they'd come over and run away with the conversation, taking it right into the safe zone of topics.

There wasn't much of a reaction to the name Trey Thompson, other than an "Oh, that's nice."

"Oh, Nala from *NYC High* is a dance student here," Caty said.

"Oh."

"My dad works on set and knows Trey pretty well," said another girl.

"Oh again," I said, my words echoing into my cup of lemonade right before I sipped. "Hey, is Miss Desi here?"

They told me she'd left. I took a seat in front of the mirrors on the floor and ate the rest of my slice in silence. It was cool hanging out in this familiar space again and seeing faces I used to see a few times a week. But, strange to say, time hadn't stopped like I imagined it would. When I thought of this place from Florida, I realized I was imaging it as it was, not the way it became after I'd left. New elite team, new traditions, new instructors. It was hard to keep up.

A song I didn't know came on and everyone squealed.

"Our song!" Eliza said, putting down her plate of food and running to the center of the dance floor. "The Bumblebee!"

I watched them do a line dance to something I'd never heard before. As odd as its title was, the song had a catchy beat. I could've jammed to this. That is, if I still lived here and went to my old studio and knew the dance moves and was a part of things.

Then Eliza waved me up. I shook my head no.

"We'll teach you!" Eliza ran over and pulled me up with two hands. Oh, okay. It took a few rounds, but I got it. Then, when the chorus started, I had to crack up. Out of the blue, they all started saying, "Bzz, bzz. Bzz, bzz," and doing some sting movements. Everyone committed.

After a few more cycles through the line dance, I was buzzing right along with everybody else.

"That was so awesomely cheesy," I said when the song was over. I was still grinning about everyone buzzing. I had to show the Squad this dance. It would be fun to bring home something new and fresh from the NYC area. I'd be an early adopter. It probably would be hitting Florida.

"I'm glad to hear you say that," said Kelly.

"Oh, really? Why's that?" I took the bait. "Do you know the singer?"

"Ew, no." She scoffed. "If I did, I wouldn't tell anyone."

I was confused. I thought everyone liked the song.

"No, it makes me happy to hear you say that because today's theme is Cheesy Party, and I was responsible for planning it. The extra-cheesy pizza and cheese balls, the cheesy song . . . Did I nail it?" Kelly asked.

This party was . . . a cheese theme?

"So how do you all know it?" I tried a different in with her.

"Well, the song is from my little sister," Kelly said. "But the cheese thing is from a comp we did a while back. Something happened, and someone said, 'so, cheese,' instead of 'oh, please,' and . . . well, I guess you had to be there." She and Eliza both laughed.

The talk turned to their latest stuff at the dance studio. Funny things that had happened without me. Crazy things that had happened without me. Annoying things that had happened without me.

By the time Eliza's mom poked her head in and told me it was time to commute back to the city, I was not bummed about leaving before the party ended. I hugged Eliza good-bye and told her I'd see her in the morning. I'd been happy to see her. Hanging out with her felt normal. But the party—all of it was based on an inside thing I wasn't a part of. That was a bit much.

When I got back to the hotel, I thanked Eliza's mom, and Riley's mom met me in the lobby to walk me up.

"I hope you had fun," she said. "But everyone else is in bed. Tomorrow is an important day. One of the dance teams is going to be crowned number one. The grand champion. The big cheese."

"Please don't say 'cheese,'" I mumbled.

*L*ily was already asleep when I got back to the hotel room that night. And on the morning of the competition, she woke up before me.

"Good morning!" I called out to her through the bathroom door. I learned Lily was big on having whole conversations through that bathroom door. As soon as she'd jump out of the shower, she'd start telling me some long, funny story, as if we'd been sitting in the same room. But this time, I could only make out a murmur in reply. That was strange. So far, it seemed Lily had been a morning person.

Could be competition jitters? I pulled my things together

as I waited for her to come out of the bathroom. I want to make sure I had everything I need in my dance bag:

Hairspray

Extra leo

Bobby pins

Tights

Hairbrush

Bandages

Tape for my feet

Water bottle

A chewy cranberry granola bar

Towel

Deodorant

Stretch band

Hair elastics!

We'd been through this once already. Did it get any easier on day two of competition? The churning of my stomach hadn't started yet. In some ways, I could be a little less confident now that we knew just how fantastic our challengers were. But then, the fact I'd already been through this the day before, so I was familiar with how it felt to go to nationals, be on a nationals stage, and compete at our best, balanced all that worry out.

And when I figured the cure for day-two jitters was to not

be here for day two, that made me feel better. Megan had been keeping up with Isabella's social media posts, so we already knew that she was back in Florida after having been bumped out of the competition. Nope. These day-two jitters were a good problem to have.

"Hey!" I perked up when Lily walked out, dressed in our fuchsia competition bodysuit. "Ready for day two?"

"Sure," Lily said without an ounce of enthusiasm in her voice. Uh-oh.

"Is everything okay?" I asked her.

"Gee. Why do you ask?" She finally gave me a little eye contact, but I almost wish she hadn't. The look in her eyes was accusing, like I was guilty of something.

"Um, I don't know, you seem a little . . . annoyed," I said hesitantly. "I know it's a stressful day. Do you want to talk about it?"

Lily put down her hairbrush and puffed out a sigh. She rolled back her shoulders, as if she was trying to work out a knot in her muscles. That must've done the trick, because after, she seemed to lighten up.

"You know what?" she asked. She rolled her shoulders again, but this time did one of Jackie and Miguel's body roll, pop, and lock moves after. "I think I'm good now."

"Just like that?"

"Mom says to shake off bad feelings," Lily said. "She's big on sleeping off your worries instead of sleeping with your worries. Also, we only have five minutes. No time to really deal with this . . ."

"And now you're literally shaking things off," I finish her thought.

"Yes." She smiled a sad smile. "For now."

I got it. I went in the bathroom to wash my face and hands before I left. Then I realized what I'd forgotten last night. That nagging feeling I had last night before meeting Eliza? That thing that I forgot to do before leaving? It was say good-bye to Lily before I left.

I looked in the mirror at the cold water dripping off my face in big droplets. Ugh. So that was why she'd been so mopey this morning. Ugh. I imagined her telling me one her postshower stories, talking on and on and not realizing she'd been talking to herself until she'd opened the door and found the hotel room empty. Empty because I'd left to go see my old friend.

Great going, Harper.

Back in the dressing room, we easily scored the same corner to camp out in. There were fewer contestants here than yesterday. The extra breathing room was nice, but there was also extra pressure in all the uncrowded air. In a few minutes, we'd all meet Vanessa in the warm-up room to work on our dance number again. It was a must. Only one team would be going home with the nationals winning title, so we had to be better than the best.

When Eliza and her elite Dance City team walked in a few minutes after us, I could feel Lily, Megan, Riley, and Trina giving me the side eye. It was as if they'd expected me to reunite with her by running across the wide room, arms wide open and ugly crying with happiness. Eliza and I exchanged glances and gave each other a hello wave, but we stayed where we were.

"Wow, where was the whole *oh, this is the biggest reunion of our lifetime!*?" Riley asked, seemingly pleasantly surprised by my actions—or, in this case, my inaction.

I pursed my lips at Riley but didn't answer. Yes, I'd been feeling guilty about what I did to Lily. But I still didn't think there was anything wrong with me being happy to see Eliza yesterday.

"Welp, you spoke too soon, Riley," said Megan, looking over my shoulder at the scene behind me. "Your bestie wants to talk to you, Harper."

Wha—? At first I didn't turn around. I thought she was stirring up drama. But then Lily pointed her chin in Eliza's direction, which confirmed it true. I turned around and saw Eliza looking back at us and waving me over.

"You're not actually going to go over there," Megan challenged when I shifted my weight to the foot pointed in Eliza's direction.

"It'll only take a second," I said. I paused. "It's not like I'm selling our dance secrets to her. She was my friend. She *is* my friend, I mean!"

"It's not about the time it would take." Megan released an annoyed chuckle. "It's about—"

Riley puts out a hand, gesturing for us to stay calm. "What she means is, you shouldn't be hanging with her this hard when the competition is so tight." I could tell by the way she said it that Riley wasn't just translating Megan's feelings, but her own, too.

I didn't want to disappoint her or anyone else on this team, but I thought they were all overreacting. *Should I stay? Should I go? But Eliza's waiting. I'd hate to let her down. But the Squad is staring, waiting for me to make a decision they would respect.* How could I choose?

Feeling tugged on both sides, I was thinking that there

was no good choice. So I turned around and walked toward Eliza, and then straight by her, out the changing room, down the hall, and right to the ladies' room. When I glanced back, I saw everyone—Lily, Megan, Riley, Trina, and Eliza— standing with their arms crossed, looking at me.

This was as stressful as the competition. Had I really just blown off my old friend? Had I also made my new friends mad? I hid in the bathroom for at least five minutes. I needed to focus. I needed to just dance. I would be dancing onstage soon. Nothing else would matter. NOTHING. *Pull yourself together, Harper*, I said to myself. *Get back in there.*

When I walked back into the dressing room, the Squad looked up from their various stretching positions. I ignored all the eyes on me and started warming up too. I sat down and began my leg stretches.

"Squad!" Vanessa said. "Join me."

We gathered around her.

"This is all stored in your muscle memory," Vanessa said. "I don't have to remind you of any of this. But I will anyway:

"Lily, you're overreaching. Be careful to show those elegant lines judges love to see.

"Megan, step over to the right on your partner trick—you're blocking Riley.

"Trina, watch your facials. You looked a bit stressed.

"Harper. Watch that footwork." Vanessa looked at me, and I nodded. "Make it look easy."

We each were wearing a numbered bib, pinned on our backs for the judges' sakes. They would be grading our individual strengths and deciding which of us would return.

Group dance time!

The team that took third place, the Scottsdale Steppers, suddenly jumped up and ran out the door in a flurry. They were up! Soon, it would be us!

We didn't get to see Scottsdale Steppers perform. Our view was blocked by extra curtains. The handler shuffled us into the wings only mere minutes before we were going to dance.

"Let's give it up for the Scottsdale Steppers!" We could hear Trey Thompson's voice. I looked over at Riley, but she seemed to not even register Trey Thompson's presence. We were that focused. I didn't like the feeling of sitting in a boiling pot of emotions. The Steppers' jazz music kicked off loudly.

"Okay, let's focus on us," Megan said. We all huddled to do our ritual.

"Dance!" Trina led the cheer. But without her usual enthusiasm, and her voice was shaking.

Lily, Megan, Trina, Riley, and I all did our little dance move—halfheartedly.

"Starz!" Trina continued.

We fluttered our fingers like sparkling stars. Then we leaned into a huddle and said:

"Squad!"

"Okay, I have to interrupt this ritual!" Vanessa surprised us backstage. "That was the weakest one I've ever seen."

"We're nervous," I confessed.

"Way beyond," Lily added. Everyone else chimed in: "Terrified. Stressed out. About to throw up."

"Of course you are," Vanessa said. "But you're ready. I know you've got this. Take it from the top."

"Dance! Starz! Squad!"

And then Vanessa surprised us as she held out her hand, palm down. "On three!" We stacked our hands on top of hers, one by one. Vanessa started us off: "One, two, three—"

"Squad!" we all shouted. All of us except Vanessa. She said something entirely different, though no one was sure what. All I could make out was that it was something with two syllables.

"Just so you all heard me," said Vanessa, a glint of mischief in her eye, "I said, 'HAVE FUN!'"

I looked blankly at Vanessa for a second to get her meaning.

What had happened to her ongoing pep talk on going harder, nailing each little step, getting it perfect? I guess she thought we'd done that. Nothing left to do but have fun.

Lily put her hand out, palm down. Vanessa stacked hers, followed by the rest of us.

"On three," said Lily. "One, two three—"

And this time, we all said the same thing: "HAVE FUN!"

Trina hopped up and down, Jackie and Miguel style. And just like that we chanted and jumped until—

"Please welcome back the Squad from Florida's Dance-Starz Academy!" Trey Thompson extended his right arm in our direction, and we jogged onto the stage, waving and cheering. The bright and sparkly fuchsia we wore only leveled up the energy. Our high-spirited arrival got the audience extra excited. They jumped and cheered along with us when the beat dropped. Some of them even got out of their seats.

The lyrics of the song we were dancing to were positive and catchy.

We dance together/We laugh together
You're a good friend
We dance forever/We laugh whenever
Never will it end

We exploded into our routine, dropping down to the floor and then springing back up in a fraction of a second, the way Vanessa trained us to do. We mirrored each other's steps perfectly. It was like we were different extensions of the same body, controlled by one brain. We had the routine down. Now was the time to have fun with it.

We made eye contact with one another, smiled at one another. It was no longer just about the judges or about the audience. It was about us, dancing and having fun. And it was contagious. More people from the audience stood up and danced along. And I could bet anything that underneath that fancy white tablecloth, the judges were probably tapping their feet too.

Speaking of feet, I was so caught up in the fun we were having, I'd already made it past the footwork routine I'd needed to improve. And I couldn't believe my ears, but the audience had learned the catchy chorus and was singing along with it. My heart tingled. It was an amazing feeling. When I looked at Trina, she already had a tear glistening in her eye. No huge surprise there. Trina was obsessed with every sappy holiday movie in existence, which she watched on her laptop with a box of tissues. But the song wasn't over. There was one final move, and we needed to be clear-eyed and tear-free to pull it off without injury.

It was the crisscross leap move. Lily, paired with Megan, and Trina, paired with Riley, had to—in two diagonal patterns like an *X*—cross each other's paths in midair and inches apart. They'd start off with a running leap, which was a lot harder than it sounded. Also, their pacing and leg extensions had to be timed right to pull the move off without knocking into one another. Not to mention, I had to time my move perfectly or I'd mess up the entire sequence. I would be doing my signature spin center stage, while moving from the back of the stage to the front. The trick was to use the music breaks as cues.

I danced my way to the back of the stage, where I positioned myself for my epic whirl-a-twirl. Trina, Lily, Megan, and Riley were at the four corners of an imaginary square, ready to take the leap. There was the musical cue! I started spinning, spotting the floodlight at the end of the ballroom while my body twisted to set each spin in motion. The trouble with turning this fast was that you were not aware of the things happening around you. I didn't know if Lily and Megan had leapt into each other, or whether Trina's eyes were too blurred with tears to be perfectly in sync with Riley. All I felt was the activity onstage. There was even a rush of wind on either sides of me, most likely kicked up by the run-up to the leap. But as I got to the front of the stage, the crowd erupted with this joyful amazement. That's when I knew.

We'd nailed it! Again!

We ran backstage with thunderous applause still raining down.

"YESSS!" I said, and Lily practically leapt into my arms. The Bunheads were jumping around together, and then they ran over and enveloped us in a huge hug. We were giddy with relief and happy tears. Then I noticed Eliza and the Dance City crew standing right behind Vanessa.

There was a brief and awkward silence, where I was still being smushed by my team, with Eliza standing there.

Then Eliza came right up to us and gave me a double high five.

"That was beyond incredible," she said. I let myself breathe then, grateful to Eliza for breaking the ice. Then she turned to my team.

"You make an outstanding team." She smiled at everyone.

"Wow, thank you so much!" Trina said. "We didn't see yours, but I'm sure it was great, too."

"I agree!" I said. "I totally do."

Eliza gave me a big hug,

Megan looked away from us, and everyone else talked

politely with one another until we were all invited back onstage.

Trey Thompson threw back a smile as we piled in. "As our top three dance troupes make their way back on stage, let's show them some New York City love and congratulate them on a fantastic job on this nationals stage today."

The applause filled my ears. I definitely felt the love. I was also feeling the butterflies. Plenty of them!

16

Unlike yesterday, when we held hands in anticipation of group qualifier announcements, there was no hand-holding going on at this moment. Lots of hand-wringing, sure. But that was it. We were totally in the moment.

"Trey looks amazing," Riley breathed.

Trey Thompson was wearing a flashy jacket today. He paired a retro baseball bomber with his blue jeans and work boots. Only thing was, his bomber and the cool swirly lettering on it was made entirely in shiny sequins. And yes, he looked great. "Judges, I don't envy the tough job you have had today." Trey gestured to the panel of five people seated flush to the stage, in front of where the corral of performers sat yesterday. "So, please—a round of applause for the judges, too."

The crowd applauded politely, as did all of us onstage. It was nice to have the attention take a break from us. The spotlight beaming on us literally shifted to the judges. But then, just as quickly as it was gone, it was back. I stood up taller and smiled.

"Now," Trey announced with a backward glance at us, "before we announce the winning group from today's amazing performances, let's see these beautiful trophies!"

Everyone oohed and aahed. Augh, I could hardly take the suspense anymore. I knew he was building it on purpose for the excitement, but I was about to explode. Finally, he said it.

"Now, here is the moment these talented performers have been waiting for. The judges have tallied their scores, and we are ready to announced the forty-fourth annual nationals winning dance group!"

The crowd seemed to collectively sit up and move to the edge of their seats. I for one was glad that the solos announcements were out of the way. It was on to the team awards—something we were all in together. I could tell the difference this made. Slowly, I could feel Lily and Trina's shoulders pressed close to mine as we all gravitated closer to each other for support. And then one of us must have been the first to reach out and take the hand of the person next to them, because it started a chain reaction until we all were holding hands.

"Nah, just kidding!" Trey said.

We all croaked a collective groan.

"Your boyfriend sure is super chatty," Trina whispered to Riley.

"I know—what is he trying to do, kill us with suspense?" Lily asked under her breath.

Trey introduced last year's winning dance team. We watched last year's group dance winners step onstage wearing Santa hats and waving to the crowd.

"Were they even competing this year?" Megan wondered aloud.

"I don't recognize them," I replied.

"No, they didn't compete this year for some reason," Riley said, like she'd just Googled it.

"No wonder they look so relaxed and stress-free."

Riley knew what she was talking about. She'd studied the roster of the winners from the last few years. She'd even noticed a few patterns and shared her observations with us over dinner one night.

"Without further ado, the envelope, please," Trey said,

probably wishing to himself that he had a live drummer on hand to add even more suspense.

One of last year's winners took an envelope and passed it to the dancer next to her, and so on, until Trey held it in his hand.

"Here we go!" Trey tore through the envelope in no time, thankfully. We squeezed one another's hands tighter and moved closer together. Trina even squeezed her eyes shut.

We'd come to New York City ready to compete. We'd done this, and we'd done it well. No matter whose name was called, this would be what carried me through any disappointment. I was proud of how we'd performed. And most of all, I was proud to be a member of DanceStarz Academy's Squad.

I spotted Vanessa in the crowd. She was standing and touching her fingers to her mouth, her eyes creased with anticipation and worry. When she caught me looking at her, she nodded.

Troy opened the envelope and then stared wordlessly at the name. The light danced across his sequined back.

"Oooh, this is good," he said.

"Read it!" someone shrieked from somewhere in the dark sea of the audience. Everyone cracked up, obviously feeling the same but too polite to express it. Even Trey chuckled and shook his head.

"Okay, here we go. For real now." He smiled mischievously before clearing his throat and gaining his composure. "Ladies and gentleman, the winning group of the forty-fourth annual nationals competition IS . . .

". . ."

". . . the Squad, from DanceStarz Academy!"

"We did it?" Trina asked in shock.

We all sat there for a split second as the crowd erupted.

"WE DID IT!" we all shouted back.

We jumped in a huddle like baseball players at the New York Yankees World Series (my favorite baseball team no matter where I would move!). It was unbelievable how things seemed to be happening in a dream. We jumped up and down with such a spring in our steps, I wouldn't have been surprised if our heads hit the ceiling. It felt as if electric current ran through each of us through our hands, zapping dizzying joy into us. We felt a jolt of happiness that was hard to describe.

"Congratulations to the Squad from Florida's DanceStarz Academy!"

We were near the edge of the stage, right next to Trey. There was dance music blaring from the speakers, with loud, thumping base vibrating my chest. Trey handed Megan—she was front and center and ready for this moment, and for once, I didn't judge—the gleaming, towering trophy that was to be ours from now on. It was gorgeous.

"How are we going to carry that back on the plane?" Trina asked. We all started cracking up.

Aside from the trophy, the applause, the cheers, and the flashing cameras, we were also handed bright, fragrant bouquets of blue and white flowers. Everything was happening so fast. We were ushered and arranged in a group photo with Trey in the next hot minute—so fast that Riley didn't have time to stand next to Trey. I quickly switched places so she could stand next to him in the front. She smiled at me appreciatively. She deserved that souvenir!

"And as if that isn't exciting enough," Trey said, "let's surprise all the dancers with some great news. Your coaches have been sworn to secrecy."

We all looked out at Vanessa, who looked smugly back.

Then Trey told us the huge news.

Anyone who made it to the solos round would not technically be competing against one another for a medal, trophy, or title. The solos were created to be the pressure-free last day of nationals. It was like a happy send-off for the participants and audiences. The performances were meant to follow a festive theme and get the crowd in the spirit. Traditionally, local schools were invited to watch the show. When I was in elementary school, my class had taken a class trip to nationals just for the day-three exhibition fun.

"Except . . . this year . . ."

Trey went on to explain that anyone selected to perform a solo would instantly be in the running for one of the most sought-after summer dance programs in the country—the Dance New York Summer Intensive! Recruiters would be attending our solo showcases and approaching their choice dancers with offers of a lifetime for the summer dance intensive!

"WHAT!" Everyone onstage was buzzing, just thinking about this. I'd never been this close to an opportunity like that before, and neither had most of us on this stage.

An envelope had been placed on the stool next to Trey—most likely by one of those stagehands who dressed in all black and had the superhuman ability to be invisible in plain sight. Trey took it and opened it deliberately.

"Let's introduce this nationals audience to the six dancers invited to perform at tomorrow's solo exhibition!

"From the Scottsdale Steppers, please help me congratulate

Alejandra and Amy!" The two girls covered their mouths and looked at each other, stunned.

I watched how this group congratulated the singled-out dancers. Had they hugged, high-fived, or just patted one another on the back? Had the dancers shown their medals to the other girls or just kept them to themselves after coming from taking their bow with Trey? Had the non-singled-out girls smiled widely or kept tight-lipped gracious smiles? I needed to prepare myself emotionally and physically for any circumstance. The Arizona group cheered excitedly for their winners. They hugged and high-fived Alejandra and Amy before they crossed the stage to collect their medals from Trey.

"Our next two . . . from DanceStarz Academy in Florida . . . Megan and Harper!"

Megan is Megan! Harper is . . . ME! Megan and ME won! I mean, *I* won! ME!

"Harper, get up there!" Lily smiled and practically shoved me to get up. Megan was already racing across the stage, and I followed her with a huge, stupid grin on my face.

"Congratulations," I whispered to Megan during our walk back to the Squad.

"Congratulations, Harper," she answered like she meant it.

Trina held out her hand and high-fived us on our way back to our spots. I stood there, the weight of the cool medal resting around my neck. I couldn't wait to show my parents and Hailey! Even my new friends at school from drama club would understand this big opportunity. I thought of my family, who were watching the live stream of this event right now, and I gave a special smile, hoping they'd know it was directed at them. It was ironic how coming here felt like going back home, yet when I thought of my family in Florida right, now I felt away from home at the same time. The tears threatened to spill over.

Keep looking at the sequins—the shiny, shimmery sequins, I told myself for the second time as Trey continued with the final soloists.

"Eliza and Genevieve of Dance City, congratulations and welcome to the solos competition!"

Oh, wow! The smile that spread across my face was a reflex. Everyone around me applauded politely, and I joined in. Unlike all the other winners announced so far, Eliza and Genevieve took the fabulous news in stride. Their faces beamed, and their eyes were wild with excitement, but they came short of looking surprised. They high-fived the other dancers on their team and walked together to collect their medals. On their return, they kept their heads held high. When Eliza glanced my way, I grinned giddily and nodded.

And that's a wrap!

People had started milling out, the music was playing low enough to hold a conversation and the ballroom lights were back on. We were still onstage, posing for photos and speaking to officials and reporters, who'd wanted to know a few details for their photo captions online.

"Harper, congrats!" A voice close behind me drew my attention away from a stagehand who was handing out small bottles of water to everyone. Eliza was waiting patiently.

"Ohmygosh, Eliza!" I threw my arms around her, careful not to scrape her with the flowers I'd been holding. She hugged me back.

"I'm so proud of you. You guys owned that stage. I saw the whole performance."

It meant so much to hear her say that. "Thank you!" I said, feeling choked up. "Congratulations on your solos slot! I can't believe how exciting that is!"

Eliza grinned. "You too!"

We threw our arms around each other again.

I sighed, still in disbelief. "Remember how we always imagined and hoped to compete on this level?"

Eliza shook her head. "We made so many plans."

"Remember the bucket-list plan to take a pic together on the nationals stage?" Eliza pointed. "Let's get someone to take a quick pic of us in front of that backdrop—but hold on," Eliza said, standing on her toes and craning her neck to peer over the small stage crowd. "My coach has all our phones."

Eliza caught her coach's eye and stepped away to retrieve her cell. I waited for her.

"We're missing Harper!" Lily called out from the front of the stage. When she spotted me, she frantically waved me over for a group shot with Vanessa and Trey Thompson. "Hurry up!"

Eliza was back with her phone,

"Ready?" she asked.

"I have to jump into a team pic," I said to Eliza, conflicted.

"This will only take a second," said Eliza.

"Harper, we're waiting!"

Not again.

Eliza wanted to head to the rear of the stage, and the Squad needed me up front.

Think and act fast, Harper, I said to myself, hoping to

avoid any more tension. Too late. I was in my second Eliza/ Squad standoff today. Everyone was giving me that stare, like they'd bet on what I'd do next. I couldn't exactly escape to the bathroom like I did last time. I made up my mind. The Squad came first. This was our moment, and I couldn't let that slip by.

"I'll be right back," I said to Eliza.

I walked away before Eliza could react, because I knew I could be guilted into changing my mind. Leave it to me to want to play both sides of the fence. I just wanted everyone to be satisfied. But easier said than done.

"Yay! Here comes Harper," cheered Trina.

"Can I get you to stand next to your coach?" the photographer had me fill the last empty spot.

We stood almost like a class picture. The trophy was on the floor, flanked by Riley and Trina, who were both kneeling on one knee. Behind them stood Lily, Megan, and me. And on either side of us were Vanessa and Trey Thompson.

Riley was looking up at Trey Thompson. This picture was going to be entertaining, at least.

The photographer put up one hand. "Everybody say 'nationals group champions!'"

"NATIONALS GROUP CHAMPIONS!" we all said.

"Trey, do you want to give me your number," Riley asked, "so I can send you a copy of the picture?"

"I think the tournament will handle that," Trey's manager jumped in out of nowhere. "Sorry, Trey has to go! He's appearing at the opening at a shoe store."

"Good-bye, Trey Thompson!" Riley called out dramatically. Trey disappeared quickly. He was not the only person who disappeared.

One second, Eliza had been watching our photo shoot while she waited on me, her phone in hand. But the next time I looked up, she was gone. I didn't see her anywhere on the stage. It hurt that she'd decided not to wait for me to take our dream photo.

"Girls! Girls! So exciting!" Megan's mom and Riley's mom had navigated their way from the large crowd, through security, and made it up onstage. They were greeted by their daughters with joyful, excited hugs. I watched their sweet hugfest. It was a precious moment, getting congratulated by their proud moms. I missed my mom, but knew I'd be getting a similar hug once I was back home.

Minutes later, we were in the dressing room, gathering our things and throwing on our team track suits.

"So, what happened to Eloise?" Megan asked, smirking. "Or wait, Elena? Elise? What's her name."

"You know it's Eliza," I said, rolling my eyes. "And I don't know. Actually."

"I thought you two were attached at the hip," Megan said.

Lily's face dropped. I opened my mouth and tried to make a comeback, something to shut down Megan and perk up Lily, but Vanessa popped in happily.

"Celebration dinnertime. We're going to eat someplace fun and different to celebrate!" Vanessa said.

"Yes!" Riley clapped and did a little hop.

"Fun, right Lily?" I tried. She didn't really respond.

"Okay, let's go upstairs to shower and change. We'll meet in our shared hall in about a half hour," Vanessa said.

"Sounds good!" we said.

"Just one request," said Riley nudging me. "When you make the reservations, can you request a seat for one more person?"

Was this a setup for an Eliza-the-fifth-wheel joke?

I wished Vanessa hadn't taken the bait. "And who would that be?"

Wait for it. I prepared myself to apologize to Lily for this one.

"Our trophy," Riley cracked herself up. "I call him Trey-phy Trophy Thompson."

Ha, okay, that was funny. We all cracked up again.

Her idea was totally silly, but her point was clear. We had a new symbol for our shared experience as members of the Squad. And like the memories we were creating together, we wanted to take it everywhere we went.

CHAPTER

17

*W*elcome to the New York City subway system!"
Vanessa stopped us so we could take yet another
group selfie outside the subway sign that said ROCKEFELLER
CENTER.

"We're taking the subway?" Megan asked, disturbed. "Can't
we walk to the restaurant?"

It was true: Every place we'd gone up until then had been
within walking distance. And I wasn't talking New Yorker
walking distance, because that would easily be twenty- and
thirty-block walks. This neighborhood had so many attrac-
tions within it and nearby, we hadn't ventured out of it and
hadn't even noticed or minded.

"There are other areas to explore!" Vanessa responded, her words forming white puffs in the cool air.

"And it's kind of the coldest day it's been so far, and I heard the subways are nice and warm," said Riley, pulling up her coat collar. She looked like a turtle ready to hide its head in its shell.

"Yeah, I'm sure that warm air is pretty healthy and clean," retorted Megan with an eye roll.

"Great, Megan," said her mom, checking her cell phone screen. "The picture caught you mid–eye roll. Let's do it one more time."

Megan wore a scowl in the next picture, but we figured it was better than the eye roll, so she didn't take another.

"How about a taxi?" Megan begged. "A car service? We deserve a limo after our big win!"

With each step we took into the subway, the street noise faded and the cold air was replaced by that old, familiar, kind of gross subway smell.

"I can already tell it's going to be humid," said Trina.

"I'm just glad it's not cold down here," Riley said, coming out of her turtle shell by letting her coat collar fall. "But ew, what's that smell?"

"It's not as bad as it would be if we came in the summer-time," Vanessa said. She seemed pretty skilled at buying us each MetroCards from the vending machine. She pressed buttons rapid-fire, even as she kept talking. "There's a stronger scent when it's hot out, for sure."

"Watch where you step," said Megan's mom as she and Riley's mom helped Vanessa buy and hand out the Metro-Cards.

"What do you mean by that?" Megan asked, clearly spooked. She looked at the floor around her, wincing.

"Only that there probably can be anything from creepy crawlers to gross garbage where you step," said Trina matter-of-factly. "My aunt had a rat run across her foot once. That's not even the grossest story she told."

"Oooh, really?" asked Riley, totally interested. "Tell us the grossest story she's told you."

"Um, no, thanks!" Megan holds up her hand to stop Trina from saying any more. "I've heard enough."

"So have I." Megan's mom wrinkled her nose. "Can we reconsider the car service?"

"No," Vanessa said sternly.

MetroCards in hand, we were ready to swipe, walk through the turnstyle, and start our journey.

There were a lot of people standing on the platform heading downtown. Lily, Trina, and Riley decided to study the subway map posted on an information board. Vanessa started chatting to the moms about the summer she'd spent interning and taking dance classes in New York.

I was surprised to see Megan walk up to me. "Did you catch the subway a lot when you lived up here?"

"Not that much," I said. "My parents would sometimes drive in and we'd walk from there. But when we did ride the subway, it was cool."

"I don't see what's so cool about it." Megan shrugged, aiming to look bored and unimpressed, but not one hundred percent convincingly.

"Don't you think it's something you can't miss seeing when you visit New York?"

"I could do without it, " she said as coolly as she could. "I don't like to to be with, uh, the masses. Underground seems beneath it all. You know?"

A blast of hot air entered the tunnel with a force, which startled Megan and obliterated her cool.

"What—? What's happening?" she asked, looking around her. She watched the train arrive like it would run out of space to stop in time. Nothing in her face seemed to scream, *Fun!*

Ah, I thought. I recognized this side of Megan from our flight in. She's scared.

"Let's go, girls!" Vanessa called, leading us onto the train. She held the doors just in case they attempted to close before we were all on.

Thankfully, for Megan's sake, we all found seats, and we were only a few stops from our destination.

As she sat rocking side to side with the motion of the express train flying through tunnels, Megan plugged into her music and closed her eyes.

"Sweetie? Are you all right, honey?" her mother asked, concerned that her daughter wasn't joining in with our chatty conversation about movies and TV shows we could think of that were filmed in real or fake New York subway systems.

"Not counting those holiday movies you're always watching," Lily said to Trina.

"No fair!" She grinned.

"I'm okay," Megan said, hanging on to the pole for dear life. Then she squinted her eyes. "Is that . . ."

We all followed her gaze. There, sitting on a seat wearing headphones, was a celebrity influencer we all recognized.

"It is," Megan breathed.

"Down here with the masses," Riley pointed out.

Megan's whole attitude shifted. Hopefully, this meant she'd be more pleasant over dinner, I thought.

"Welcome to the legendary Greenwich Village!" said Vanessa with a flourish in her hand as we exited the subway and made our way aboveground.

We oohed and aahed our way around the neighborhood, exploring the shops, the architecture, and the epic people-watching.

"Now, this is my type of area," said Megan, admiring the uniqueness of everything she laid her eyes on. "Fancy."

"Does that mean the subway trip was worth it?" I teased her.

"Duh, of course," Megan said. "All real New Yorkers take the subway."

It was good to see her feeling better. Even if that meant I'd have to keep a sharp eye and ear out for her shady remarks.

"Well, when you try the food at the restaurant we're going to, you'll agree it was all worth it," said Vanessa.

And she was totally right. I'd never had Turkish food before. The chicken kebab plate I ordered was so good! Like, how could I have made it through life without this delicious-ness? I felt like calling my parents and demanding they answer that question. I pulled out my phone to take a picture of my food. Then I paused.

I'd missed two texts while we were underground: from

my dad and from Zora asking me how New York was. Which made me realize: Eliza still hadn't returned my text messages. I'd sent her three. In the first one, I'd asked where she'd gone. I mean, I'd thought she'd wait for me to finishing taking those team photos. But when I'd looked up, she'd disappeared. The next text was to send her a link to an article posted on a dancers' website about the nationals that featured a photo of Dance City midperformance. And the third text was sent just to ask her if she was okay. It wasn't like her to ghost me like that.

She really must've been ghosting me on purpose.

Eliza must have been sitting all in her feelings about my walking away from that photo, and the thought made me feel uneasy.

"What's the matter, Harper? Is it the food?" Vanessa asked.

"No." I tried to laugh it off and play it cool. "The food is amazing."

"Well, finish up, because we want to get in enough time hanging out at the rink."

"We have to leave already?" Megan asked. "Wait, does the subway run at night? Is it really dark down there?"

"We can take a taxi back," Vanessa told her.

"Whew!" Megan burst out. "I mean, okay, cool."

"But first, a toast. Here's to the most talented, hardest-working team I've ever had the pleasure of taking to nationals," said Vanessa.

"Hear, hear!" the moms replied, bursting with pride. This was a big moment for them, too.

Together with all of our parents, they were our number one fans.

No one celebrated our wins like they did. I was so grateful to my parents and to Hailey for cheering me on every step of the way, all the way to nationals.

"Riley and I came up with a fabulous idea to celebrate," Riley's mother said.

Riley picked up a spoon and pretended it was a mic.

"DanceStarz Squad, you've just earned top honors at the forty-fourth annual dance nationals. What are you going to do now . . . since we're outside of Florida and too far from Disney World?"

"We're going ice-skating!" she announced. "At the famous rink at Rockefeller Center!

"Well . . ." Vanessa held up a finger. "Not all of you can skate. Sorry, Megan and Harper, but you know the rules. No risky activities before competition."

Ugh. I knew that rule was meant to protect us.

"Oh dear, I hadn't thought of that," Riley's mother said.

Vanessa caught sight of Megan's pout. "No exceptions."

"Well, now my daughter is left out of the celebration?" Megan's mother frowned at Riley's mother. Uh-oh.

"It's fine!" Megan and I both said quickly.

"I guess you both have to watch from the sidelines, the way we'll be watching you both tomorrow," said Trina, smiling.

"That's fair." I smiled back at her. Actually, it made me feel better about my solo privilege knowing that the rest of the squad would enjoy a special outing like this. "Megan and I can cheer you guys on. We can get hot chocolate, right, Vanessa?"

"Definitely," Vanessa said, smiling.

"Megan, they have the best hot chocolate at the rink," I said. "It's like drinking a melted candy bar."

"That does sound yummy." Megan gave in. Her mother relaxed too.

We made our way to the rink, which was still pretty busy, even at night. Megan and I hung out with the rest of the squad as they rented ice skates. After they laced up their classic white skates, Lily and Trina handed us their phones like we were their personal photographers.

Trina and Lily were on the ice first.

"This place is so cool! I can't pay attention to where I'm going when the view is so distracting!" Trina said.

This had to be the best place in the city to see the holiday lights—especially when the sun was going down like it was now. The decorated Christmas tree stood high above the rink like some special guest from a gigantic magical forest. It was so gorgeous. And the famous bronze statue of Prometheus at the level below the tree was not bad on the eyes either. It was a shimmering sight and surrounded by a water feature you could stare at all day. Plus, those holiday lights. They were everywhere and on everything lining the plaza. I remembered when I had my own ice skates and used to skate on the pond near our neighborhood.

"I forgot how much I love to ice-skate," Lily said to Trina as she skated by. "I don't think about it as much in Florida. I can usually go to the beach in the winter, not an outdoor rink!"

"Nice!" I said, leaning over the rail to snap a few pics of Lily's graceful glides. Megan stood next to me, reluctantly aiming Trina's cell phone at Trina as she cautiously made her way around the rink. She was kind of gliding/stepping her way around the outer part of the rink, hanging on to the boards.

"C'mon, do something worth taking a picture of," Megan teased Trina. Trina paced a bit away from the railing herself and waved at the camera.

"Where's Riley?" I asked, looking around.

Trina chimed in. "Yeah, anyone seen Riley? She was with us when we were putting on our skates."

Just then, Vanessa and Riley's mom skated by, arm in arm.

"Aw, look how cute that was!" Trina squealed.

"Riley's not with Vanessa or the moms," I said, craning my neck toward the outdoor seating.

"She's wearing black, so it'll be tough to find her in this crowd," said Lily, peering over the crowd.

"There she is!" said Trina, like she'd found Waldo.

Sure enough, Riley was halfway down the rink, pulling herself up from her hands and knees.

"She must have wiped out pretty bad," said Megan, smirking.

"I'll go help her," said Lily. But before she could reach her, Riley started sliding uncontrollably toward Trina.

"Whoa, here I come!" a wide-eyed Riley shouted.

"Watch out!" Lily shrieked, but Riley slammed right into Trina anyway. It was a good thing Trina was still close to the guardrail, otherwise the both of them would've been dropped.

"Are you guys okay?" I reached out and gripped Riley's arm in case she hadn't yet regained her balance.

"We're okay. Yup, okay," Trina said. "Just a little out of control."

Megan, Lily, and I made sure they were both fine before we started cracking up at the timing of Riley's body slam.

"Trina's getting better on those skates!" I remarked after watching her effortlessly skate around Riley.

"Oh, yeah?" said Lily, tying her scarf and fixing her knit hat in place. "Bet she can't do this!" She did some fast back crossovers, and a little twirl at the end.

My mouth swung open. Who knew Lily could move like that on the ice? That was just another small reminder that I had so much to learn about Lily.

"Lily, you're so good at skating!" I yelled to her. I could tell that no matter what tension was between us, she liked that compliment. She turned around and began skating backward. As I took a video of her, I was beginning to see how I'd taken her for granted since we'd come to New York. Leaving to go hang with Eliza without letting her know I was doing that in the first place was one major goof that stood out in my mind. I hoped to be a better friend to her. Lily kicked up a good speed and then put her back leg up in a banana-split pose before skating away like a pro. A few skaters offered their muffled applause, and Lily took a dramatic bow.

"Is that all you've got?" I shout, grinning.

"Easy for you to say on solid ground. But give me a move to do and I'll match it!" Lily challenged me playfully.

Any move I thought up would look a lot more amazing on ice, thanks to Lily's skill level. I did a sample of today's winning routine. Because I could hear Vanessa's warning in my ear, I didn't want to cause Lily any extra risk while her lower body was weighed down by those rented skates. Instead, I overemphasized the arms and head chorco. There was holiday music playing on the plaza speakers, and I danced along with the tunes like this was the Olympic trials.

Megan, Lily, and Trina recognized the moves right away and chuckled. "Nice!"

As soon as I was done, Lily extended her arms and gracefully skated through the moves with the wind whipping through her hair. She looked like an ice goddess!

"You guys have nothing on me!" Trina was back, but with Riley literally hanging on to her coattails. "Watch this!"

"Oh, boy." Megan playfully rolled her eyes as Trina gestured to her to get the camera ready.

"Wait, wait, wait!" Riley let go of Trina's coat hem and made her way, clumsily, to the guardrail. "I didn't say go fast!"

We grinned to ourselves and gave Trina the stage. She

pushed off slowly but elegantly and took a wide turn and came back toward us before turning off again.

"She's making a figure eight! See it?" Lily pointed at the lines Trina's blades had etched into the ice.

"Whoa! I did not expect that," Megan said when Trina joined us again, taking a bow midglide.

"Okay, me next, me next!" said Riley, raising her hand like she was in class.

We all looked at each other. "Uh, are you sure, Riley?"

A new guest DJ must've just reported to work, because the holiday music disappeared, and the next song was more pop with a sick bass.

"I love this song!" Riley clapped and bobbed up and down in place. She boldly skate-walked closer to the railing, her arms pumping. When she was close enough to grab the railing with both hands, she began hopping and landing on the toe of one skate and the heel of another. On the spot she invented and then repeated the most intricate footwork I'd seen in a while. Riley's moves drew a small crowd.

"Fancy!" Lily cupped her hands to her face and shouted in her direction.

I gave Riley a gloved high five when she was done, a little breathless but still triumphant.

"Megan, you want to give that a try on solid ground?" I asked her.

She looked like she wanted to tie my sneaker laces to each other. "No, thanks."

Then I heard the beginning notes of something that made my heart sink for a moment. Brought back bad memories. Then I saw all of the younger kids scream and race to the center of the rink.

"What even is this?" complained Megan, leaning on the guardrail.

"That's the Bumblebee song," I said.

"The what?" Riley asked.

"It's a trendy song," I said. "The Bumblebee. I'll show you how to do it. It's a line dance thing." I faced everybody and started the dance from whatever move I remembered most. The more I got into it, the more of the dance I remembered.

Lily and Trina joined in, and we swayed in sync for a few more cycles before Riley felt comfortable enough to join in too. Megan watched from the guardrail as I went through the line dance, step by step. I repeated and repeated it again. Across the rink, a larger group had formed in a line, and they were *Bzz, bzz, bzz*-ing away.

"When I get back home, I'm going to show everyone I know that dance," Riley said.

"I think this is fun," I decided. Sure, it was cheesy, but I was happy that they liked the dance as much as I'd thought they would. "It's not fun," complained Megan from the sidelines.

"Don't be embarrassed to like it," I told her. "It's easier if you try it off the ice, of course."

"Who says I'm embarrassed? And who says I can't skate?" Megan said. "Anyway, ice-skating is dumb. Wearing someone else's borrowed shoes and going in circles on a giant ice cube? Who needs to do that? Bunheads! Are we finished here?"

Trina skated over to Riley. They linked their arms as Trina guided Riley around the rink and out the exit, where Megan met them.

That left Lily and me. We stared at their backs in silence.

"Can we talk?" I asked her.

"Sure. Okay," Lily said.

"All right, so—" I started. Just then a group of kids grabbing hands did a huge, long whip, and the kid holding at the end whipped so quickly by Lily, she almost fell over.

"Anyway," I said when we recovered from that, "I just wanted to say—"

Two couples holding hands pushed in between us, blocking my view of Lily. This was not working so well.

"Want to go get hot chocolate?" I shouted to her.

"Yeah, okay!" Lily yelled back. She weaved her way through the crowd and headed out the exit door.

We got lucky. We caught the concession stand when the line was relatively short. We had our hot chocolates a few minutes later. The warm cup felt amazing to hold. It also felt nice to sit for a moment.

"Hey, girls!" Vanessa waved to us from a few tables away, where she and the moms were chatting.

"Rad moves out there!" Riley's mother called out.

"Thank you!" We waved back.

"She's the one with the skills!" I pointed at Lily.

"When I get home," I said to Lily, "I'll have to find a skating rink I could go to every so often so I can practice to catch up to your skills."

"Connecticut home?" Lily asked.

"No, I mean Florida," I said. I paused and looked at the dazzling Christmas tree. "I know I've been weird. It's complicated, I guess. It's tough to explain. You wouldn't understand."

Lily wraps her hands around her drink. "Why would you think I wouldn't understand?"

I considered her question.

"I'm new to DanceStarz, just like you are," Lily continued. "I moved from the only home I knew too, you know. Maybe I was in the same state, but still."

"But you seem to be adjusting so great. It's like you're handling everything so well. Plus, your parents' shop feels like it's always been there," I said. "I guess you don't even talk about your old home, so for some weird reason, it feels like you're not new."

She shrugs. "Maybe I just don't show my feelings about this as much. But believe me, I know how weird and hard it is when you're new. At least you got to see your friends. I haven't been back since I moved."

"Well, I've been making it even weirder for you these past few days." I make a face. "I'm so sorry about slipping out of our room the other day without saying good-bye."

"Yeah, that was super weird and uncool," said Lily. "When Eliza is around, it's like you forget you have other friends."

I knew this was the point the others—especially Megan—had been trying make to me these past few days, but hearing it from Lily was like the kick in the pants I needed.

I winced. "That bad, huh?"

Lily crossed her arms and nodded.

"I'm so sorry." I let out a deep sigh. "That was totally uncool. You shouldn't have had to deal with that. I was just so excited to be here and fit back into my old life, I think I lost my way."

"Well, now I feel bad I didn't ask." Lily uncrossed her arms and leaned her elbows on the little round tabletop. "How was your visit in Connecticut?"

"It was nice, but not what I'd imagined it would be." I leaned forward too, resting my forearms on the table. "Before I visited, I thought that I would just go to Connecticut and pick up where I left off. But so much had changed. And for a while there, I was confused about where I belong."

I told her about my "cheesy" night.

"Yikes."

I nodded. "They weren't doing anything on purpose. I just felt left out in my own head. And I didn't mean for you to feel the way I felt that night."

"Thanks for saying that," Lily said, looking lighter from the weight lifted off her shoulders. It was so nice being able to talk to her honestly like this. I was glad she was willing to hear me out after all I'd done. Her phone went off. She pulled it from her jacket pocket and smiled when she looked at the screen.

"It's my parents!

"Cool!"

Lily and I said hi to her mom and dad. "The trophy is going to be held in a display case at DanceStarz Academy," Lily explained to her parents. I smiled to myself when I imagined what the look on the faces of the tiniest dancers there would be.

As she spoke to them, me waving hello in the background, I decided to video chat my own family. Hailey would love to see where I was right now. There were a lot of competing sounds around us, but I could still make out my parents' words. They said they couldn't wait to see the trophy in person.

It was sweet how excited my mom was for me. "I'm so happy this was such a great trip for you!" she said, getting a little too close to the camera. "Winning the nationals, getting a solo, seeing Eliza again . . ."

Eliza still hadn't reached out. It wasn't a good feeling knowing we were leaving things this way. But I knew I'd see her tomorrow one last time before we flew back to Florida. I hoped maybe I could make things better then.

18

*I*f we were nervous on day one and guarded on day two, day three was all about excitement.

Nationals was dropping its competitive edge and going festive for the day. We'd been invited to not only dance but watch the exhibition performers from the audience! Aside from nationals having invited all contestants still in town to come see the show, the top three dance teams were asked to make an appearance onstage in full performance gear, just like last year's winners had yesterday.

This meant that the morning of the day-three show, Lily was up and dressed early too. We were both arranging our beauty products on the hotel room desk to make it easier to get the pregame routine started.

Knock, knock, knock!

I looked at Lily. "That can't be our fifteen-minute warning already."

"It's us!" Trina whispered through the door.

Lily unlocked the door, and Trina, Megan, and Riley rushed in carrying armloads of products. "We thought it would be fun to do hair and makeup together our last day."

"That's a fun idea." I smiled from ear to ear.

"Turn on some music," said Riley to no one in particular. "Something good."

"Whose phone has the best speaker?" Lily asked.

"Megan's!" everyone agreed. Megan had a skill for getting her parents to buy her most of everything she wanted. Her tech game was on point.

"Fine, but then I get to choose the playlist," Megan said.

Before long, we were all cracking jokes and telling stories.

"You guys," I said. "I'm sorry if I made things weird with my old studio and stuff. Moving is hard."

"Aw, it's good having Harper back on our side," said Riley, adding pins to her flawless bun.

"It was never about choosing sides," Lily said in my defense. "She was just hanging out with an old friend."

"It sure looked like she was always swinging back and forth from over here," said Megan, angling her hand mirror so she could check out her updo from different angles.

"I admit I was excited to see Eliza, since I hadn't seen her in so long," I said.

"We knowwww," Riley said, rolling her eyes.

"But know that I consider you guys my new team totally, and just because I still have a good friend back home, it doesn't mean that I've forgotten who has helped me get here," I said, making eye contact with everyone, especially Lily.

"We forgive you!" Trina put down her curling iron and walked over to give me a hug. Lily threw her arms around the both of us, and then Riley joined the group hug, pulling Megan along with her.

"Squad on three!" shouted Lily from somewhere inside of the group hug. "One, two, three . . ."

"SQUAD!" we shouted before breaking away.

"National championship Squad!" I pumped my fist. We rode that team bonding feeling all the way to the backstage at nationals.

*   *   *

"Right after this performance, Trey will call you out to take a bow," said the busy stagehand who'd led us to the stage from our front-row seats moments before.

We nodded and thanked her before she speed-walked off, disappearing into the backstage scenery.

Up until now, we'd been having a great time watching Trey MC. He was wearing another sequined bomber, but I didn't need to train myself to stare into its shimming back, because the pressure was totally off my shoulders. I sat in the audience enjoying Trey's charming MC style, cheering for the exhibition performers, and tossing the balloons that at one point were released from a giant net overhead.

Between the surprise pop-up Squad salon in our hotel room to the fun show, it had been more of a chill morning. My stomach wasn't churning as loudly as it had been the past two days. That is, until I saw something that got it going again.

The stagehand was back with another person—Eliza. "Your performance will be right after they take their bow," she instructed Eliza.

There was an awkward silence for a few seconds.

"Hey, Eliza," I said as I walked over to her.

"Hey, Harper," she smiled, but she seemed a little quiet.

Everyone else greeted Eliza, except for Megan.

That was all anyone said. We turned our attention to the performance about to start onstage. Trey had just finished interviewing the little girls dressed up like rock-star elves— candy-striped leggings and Santa hats with black biker jackets. They told Trey they were kindergarteners from New Jersey.

When they started dancing to a popular holiday song, we couldn't look away from their performance. It was the cutest thing. Throughout their routine, they didn't stop smiling and engaging the audience. There were a boatload of people out there, but these little girls weren't intimidated by that at all. They gave it their all until the very last note of the song.

The crowd went wild for them.

"That was fun!" said a tiny, giggling voice. The kindergarteners were exiting the stage in our direction.

They could hardly contain their excitement. Trina put up her hand—not too high up—so that each kid could high-five her on their way off stage. It was such a sweet, supportive thing to do, so I stood behind her and did the same. Lily and Riley stood across from us, creating a tunnel of congrats for the kids. Megan and Vanessa followed suit—one stood across from the other. As the kids walked through, I looked at the tops of their heads, bobbing all the way through our tunnel.

They weren't concerned with outperforming anyone or scoring higher; they were just having fun. And their excitement was contagious.

"Have fun!" the little girl in braids shouted to us. She probably assumed we'd be heading out to dance as a group.

"Trina!" I responded, giving her a high five. "Did you hear her orders? Let's have fun!" I said, playfully pumping my fist.

"Have fun!" Lily chimed in like she was chanting.

"Have fun! Have fun!" We all grinned and continued chanting with the little girls.

Eliza stared blankly at us at first, but then seemed to blink the judgment away. She chuckled to herself and smiled.

"Ladies and gentlemen, introducing the champions of the forty-fourth annual nationals dance competition, the Squad, from DanceStarz Academy!"

We trotted our way to center stage, waving to the cheering crowd. By now it felt like Trey Thompson was an old friend.

"This group came to town and took it by storm. I have to say, as we wrap up these three days, I am a fan."

Riley jumped up and down, and we covered our mouths, laughing. That was so cool of him to say.

"You have inspired dancers such as myself to aim higher, and I thank you for being such a good example," said Trey.

"Wowzers!" Riley high-pitched shrieked to us, but Tristan's mic picked it up loud and clear. The crowd laughed but cheered Riley's relatable outburst.

Trey laughed and threw a big-brotherly arm around Riley to help her recover from her embarrassment.

"We wish the Squad all the best, and we look forward to seeing their solo performances. Let's hear it again for them!"

We waved and then exited the stage the same way we'd entered.

The stagehand was back, instructing Megan and me to stay with Eliza backstage. As the final three solo acts left, we'd have back-to-back performances, beginning with Eliza and followed by Megan and then me. Afterward, we were to run back onstage together for a quick, joint bow.

It was odd to admit it, but being alone with Megan was less awkward than being alone with Eliza right now. I was glad when it was her turn onstage. Plus, I was happy that I got to see her perform. I always love checking out her unique flow of movement. She was a naturally talented dancer who seemed like she could excel at any type of dance. She'd chosen a lyrical routine to a jazzy holiday tune, and she was out there rocking it.

"She's not bad," Megan said, her eyebrows raised.

I couldn't tell if that made Megan like Eliza more or less. Megan didn't give away any clues either way, because when Megan came out, she continued giving her the same cold shoulder.

"You were flawless out there!" I greeted Eliza, forgetting we were sort of mid–silent treatment.

"Thanks," she smiled, still charged and happy from her dance. She went and got her water bottle and took a few gulps.

"That's my cue," said Megan when Trey announced her right away.

"You got this!" I whispered to her as she sashayed to her marked spot onstage, her arms swinging side to side in the air.

Eliza and I watched in silence, standing shoulder to shoulder. I had to say something to her, now while Megan wasn't around. We'd be flying out later tonight, and I didn't want to leave things the way they were.

I cleared my throat. "We didn't get to take our picture on the nationals stage," I said, looking straight ahead.

"Oh, right! I kind of forgot about that, actually," she replied, keeping her eyes on Megan.

"You did?" I pivoted to face her. "I texted you a few times yesterday."

Eliza looked at me, puzzled. "Ack! I'm sorry! I thought I texted you back."

"Really? I thought you were mad at me!" I blurted.

Eliza stared at me, even more confused than before. "Mad? Why?"

Before I could respond, the crowd erupted in applause for Megan, who was making her way offstage with her hands up. I answered by meeting her with high fives.

"You were amazing," I said truthfully.

"I know," she responded with a mischievous grin. I shook my head and half smiled.

"Let's hear it for Harper, our next dancer from DanceStarz Academy in Florida!" Trey shouted me out.

Eek! I'd been so wrapped up in everything I'd almost forgotten it was going to be my turn to dance.

"You got this!" I heard Megan throw at my back. Well. That was unexpected and nice.

My turn to shine.

I remembered when I first moved to Florida and I was so nervous about not being good enough on my new dance squad. I remember imagining what it would like to be chosen for a solo. . . .

The announcer would say:

Please welcome to the stage: Harper! Performing . . . A SOLO!

I would walk onto the stage, my head held high. I would get into my opening pose as the music began . . . five . . . six . . . seven . . . eight! And I would dance! I would dance, and I would nail it!

Now it was really happening—at nationals! I trotted onto the stage, flashing a smile, waving at the crowd before turning my back to them. As the sleigh bells rang out in surround sound, I twisted my torso to the right to peek at the crowd playfully. I did the same to the left before launching into a barrel turn and barrel jump. It was a routine packed with tricky moves in the first part of the dance, but I felt lighter than air with each leap, kick, and spin.

But a few seconds later, as I braced myself for the tricky footwork Vanessa had drilled into me, something totally unexpected happened—just as I went into my most important turn series.

I took my prep and held my plié for a second, then pulled up, spotting—One! Two! Three! Four! Five turns! And then . . . somebody bumped a stage light.

The light dimmed for a second, then it shifted—to the shimmering sequins on Trey's jacket. Trey was sitting at the judges' panel in front of the stage, totally unaware that the floodlight bouncing off his jacket was blinding me.

HUH?

I lost my spotting at a time I'd needed to concentrate most. The sequins on his jacket were like a million tiny mirrors pointing a million tiny bright suns in my face. I froze in a panic, not knowing where I'd left off and what to do next.

What had happened to *I would dance and I would nail it*?!

It was a disaster. I was blinking into flashes of white light that I could see even when I turned away or closed my eyes. I couldn't believe this was the end to my time at nationals. My song was more than halfway over, but I wanted to run off the stage now. But I couldn't—because I couldn't see where the exits were. Usually, I would have kept going, but I couldn't do any leaps or jumps or turns—or I'd risk falling off the stage.

The audience was starting to whisper and rustle around, clearly confused by what was happening. I was so embarrassed. I couldn't move.

The music came to a screeching halt.

"Technical difficulties!" came over the loudspeaker. "Do not move. Please hold."

And then, from the nonflashing corner of my eye, I saw Eliza and Megan rush—well, not rush, more like carefully stumble into the light, to stand next to me.

"We can help you offstage!" Eliza whispered. Then she paused. "No, we can't. It's a lot brighter here than I thought."

I was so grateful to have them there.

"Thanks for being good friends," I said, shading my eyes from the light.

But then Megan took two light steps to the left and two to the right before hopping back once and making a quiet buzzing sound.

The Bumblebee dance! I'd taught it to Lily, Trina, and Riley at the rink, but Megan hadn't danced along. Apparently, though, she'd been paying attention. But why was she doing this?

Eliza joined in, and after a beat, I followed too. The crowd roared when they recognized what we were doing. Some of the younger kids in the audience jumped out of their seats and filled the aisle, doing the line dance along with us. Pumped up by all the fun, Trey removed his jacket and joined the kids in the audience to groove alongside them.

Then when the chorus started, I had to crack up. Out of the blue, they all started saying, "Bzz, bzz. Bzz bzz" and doing some sting movements. Everyone committed.

It turned out to be a party!

Trey was breathless when he came up onstage to thank us for closing out the solos together. The three of us took our bows, waved to the crowd's cheerful applause, and exited the stage one final time.

"Thank you both!" I hugged Megan and Eliza with all that I had left.

"Riley warned you that you'd eventually be blinded by Trey's charm," Megan joked.

"That she did." I laughed with Eliza.

"Harper, I wasn't mad that you didn't take the photo with me," Eliza explained. "Well, I was a little annoyed maybe, but I knew you had your team. And I really forgot to text you!"

Phew! I was so glad nothing was really wrong there. And then something else that was wonderful occurred to me as I looked at Harper and Megan. "Hey, who would've thought I'd see you two join forces?"

"We're all on the same team today," said Eliza. "Team Harper!"

"Team Harper on three!" Megan shouted, her hand held out palm down. We gladly stacked our hands. "One . . . two . . . three . . ."

"TEAM HARPER!" we shouted together, cheering and high-fiving each other.

"Now how about that photo?" Eliza asked me.

"Let's do it!" I smile from ear to ear.

After the show was over, and the audience spilled out the

ballroom, the dancers were told to wait together.

"Eliza, there's someone who wants to talk to you." Eliza's coach came over toward a man who wore a jacket that said MIAMI DANCE. While they spoke off to the side, Eliza's beaming smile and frequent head nods told me all I needed to know. I was so happy for her.

As I waited patiently, eager to hear her details, Vanessa walked over to me, smiling with her eyes. There was a woman I didn't recognize at Vanessa's side.

"Harper, this is Ms. Irving, a recruiter from Dance New York."

My stomach flip-flopped like a pancake, and I froze. DANCE NEW YORK?

"So nice to meet you," I said, trying to hold it together.

Ms. Irving shook my hand. "Harper, it is nice to meet you and to see you perform."

Gasp! Were her colleagues impressed with my deer-in-headlights routine too? I was simultaneously panicking and celebrating that Dance New York saw me perform. And choke. They saw me choke.

She smiled at Vanessa.

"She saw *all* your performances," Vanessa said, as if reading my mind. "Not just today."

"Yes, I know today's took an unusual turn," Ms. Irving

said, "but that actually wasn't a bad thing for us. We are looking for dancers to audition into our program for technique and talent, naturally. But we have students of all ages, and seeing you so engaged with the younger dancers is something that we appreciate. We believe you'd make an exceptional addition to our summer program here in New York City."

WUT. Had I really heard that?

"WUT?!" Oops, had I really said that.

"Harper?" Vanessa raised an eyebrow.

"No worries," Ms. Irving said. "I take it as a compliment."

"It is! Thank you!" I finally sputtered. "Thank you so very, very much."

"This is for your parents," said Ms. Irving, handing me a letter with the Dance New York logo on top. It was an invitation, a welcome to join their summer program! "We'll follow up with more information."

I jumped up and down before gaining my composure.

"We hope to have you join us." Ms. Irving shook my hand again before walking away.

"So do I!" I said.

"Congratulations, Harper." Vanessa gave me a hug and took a look at the letter. "I am one proud coach. First Megan and now you—today is a good day."

"Megan?"

"Yes! I'll let her share the good news."

"Wow," I said. "Coming to nationals can really change a dancer's life."

"That it can," said Vanessa. "It did for me." She winked and waved my letter in the air. "I'm going to put this is a safe place."

I watched Vanessa slip away as Eliza ran up to me with her awesome news.

"I'm invited to go to Memphis All-Stars!" she said, her eyes shining.

"Wait, what?" I said. "In Tennessee?"

"Yup. And Megan got in too . . . so I'll be spending the summer with her." Eliza paused. "Do you think she'll teach me how she does that leg-hold trick? That was impressive."

I smiled. I was a little bummed I didn't get to Megan first, but I figured I could pretend I hadn't heard her news yet!

"And I heard you're going to be in New York," Eliza said. "How funny is that I'm going south and you're coming back here?"

"Well, maybe we won't be there at the same time so I can see you when I'm here," I said. "It's just sinking in. Wow! We got scouted!"

"Can you believe we did this?!" Eliza said. We both jumped around in excitement.

In our final act on the nationals stage, Eliza and I took our position in front of the illuminated city skyline backdrop for our photo. Vanessa was kind enough to snap the pics using both Eliza's and my cameras. Eliza and I posed, arm in arm, with our knees pointed at each other.

"Okay, now try something else!" Leave it to Vanessa to comment on the choreography of anything.

Eliza and I stood back to back with one knee bent and our feet planted sole to sole. And then we got photobombed by the rest of the Squad.

"Yaaay!" they shouted, jumping in and gathering us in a huddle. We quickly arranged ourselves, arm in arm, in a straight line across the backdrop.

"I love being in New York with you all!" I shouted.

"If I can make it there—" Trina started singing.

And suddenly we were kicking Rockettes style. The official nationals photographer who had taken our group shots with Trey Thompson was now pointing his camera to us too.

"It's up to you, New York, NEW YORK!" we all sang. My old and new friends together.

There was no better way to wrap up our visit to New York City. This was the sweetest send-off I could've imagined.

CHAPTER 19

I spoke too soon. The sweetest send-off I could've imagined was the one that happened next. To make up for not inviting the Squad along the first time, I planned to pull Vanessa and the moms aside and ask if Eliza and I could take them to the famous Cupcake Queen place we went to earlier in the trip.

We had just come from the final farewell on the nationals stage and were headed to the chill room to grab our things and go. Our heads were still buzzing from the excitement of the past three days. And it was strange knowing that we would be catching a flight back to Florida in about six hours. I was excited to see my family, but of course, I would miss being in New York.

The memories we made here would always stay with me. The Squad and I had visited so many places we could reminisce about over and over again. I remembered how Trina had said she liked to go to this one cupcake place with her grandmother, and I wanted to do what I could to make a visit happen. First, I had to get the chaperones on board. Eliza was with her mom. She said her mom wanted to come to personally meet the team that would be taking home the nationals champ award.

A lot of audience members who had exited the ballroom about a half hour ago or more had apparently been hanging out in the lobby. When we exited the backstage door leading to the hall, we hadn't anticipated this. People recognized us and greeted us. As strange as it sounded, folks even asked to take pictures with us. A few little girls asked us to sign their programs. It was pretty unexpected and incredible.

In all of the activity, while Megan, Riley, Trina, and Eliza were speaking to moms, little girls, and summer program coaches, I'd managed sneak in quick side conversations with the chaperones.

"Sure," said Vanessa without hesitation when I suggested the cupcake place.

"We're fine with it if they are," said Megan's mom.

We had an evening flight to catch, but there was plenty of time to hang out. And this was exactly what I told the Squad as we packed up our bags, ready to leave the venue one last time.

"Are you doing this out of guilt? Because there's no reason to still be feeling guilty," said Lily.

"I'm doing this because I think you guys would love this place. And yes, I do feel bad for not inviting you to go with us the first time. "

"I don't understand why we're still talking about it," said Riley. "You had me at 'cupcakes.'"

"Same!" Trina nods, laughing.

"And you say Eliza is coming?" Megan asked, arms crossed.

Uh-oh. Here we go again.

"I was only asking about Eliza because she said there's this place she gets cool boots," Megan said, smiling. "I need to find out where exactly that is."

Whew. "Yay! Then it's settled. Let's drop our bags upstairs and head over!"

"This place must be magical," Lily said, her eyes darting across the colorful walls inside the cupcake place.

"That was exactly what I thought when I first came here!" I said. "Wait until you try the cupcakes."

"It's like we've walked into an animated world," said Trina.

We jumped in line before it grew any longer.

"I'll grab a tray," I said.

"Did someone say TRAY?" Riley sighed. "Like Trey Thompson?"

"I'm curious, now that you've actually met the real-life Trey Thompson," Lily asked Riley, "did he live up to your high standards?"

"Are you kidding me? Trey IRL exceeded my expectations!" Riley cooed. "I'm so happy we'll have pictures for proof. And to enlarge for my wall. And my locker."

"I'm happy for you." I laughed. We moved up in line.

"Wait until you try the cupcakes," Eliza said. "I think they, too, will exceed your expectations."

I chose a peanut butter cupcake this time, with chocolate icing. Eliza picked chocolate truffle, Lily got tie-dye, Megan got red velvet, Riley got lemon, and Trina got the black-and-white. We put them all on the tray and headed to the two tables next to a window. The chaperones sat at a nearby table with their own cupcakes and treats.

Eliza and Riley made a figure eight with the tables, and we arranged the chairs around them.

"Dig in!" I said, placing the tray in between the tables.

And then silence. The only loud things were everyone's facial expressions. Closed eyes, sneaky smiles, raised eyebrows. I'd say they were enjoying the treats.

"I have questions," said Megan, annoyed and scrolling through her phone. "I want to know why this place has not expanded its cupcake business to Florida."

"Just wrong," scoffed Riley. "And selfish."

"Well, I guess you guys are just going to have to all come back to New York." Eliza smiled.

"Wait a minute," Lily said with her mouth full. "Harper will be back here next summer. She's our in!"

"I'll be glad to bring back a case of cupcakes . . . if you can promise to be super kind and sweet to me," I said.

"For the next seven months?!" Megan almost put down her cupcake in shock. Almost.

"Is that a difficult request?" Eliza looked at us back and forth.

"Well, hello!" a man's voice I recognized called out. "Are these our out-of-towners and locals sitting together? In peace and harmony?"

"Wow, I think the answer for what ails the world is in this here cupcake shop," the woman with him added.

"Jackie and Miguel!" we shouted, so happy to see our one-time hip-hop dance instructors.

"Hey, guys!" They looked so hip, in cool hats and fashionable jackets. Miguel had switched his dancing sneakers for a pair of work boots. And Jackie was wearing a dope pair of lace-up heels.

"Funny running into you again," I said, smiling.

"They say the city is like a small town in many ways," explained Miguel. "The iced coffee is great here, and I will go far for a good iced coffee."

"Music is pretty good too," Jackie said. "Let's see what you got," Jackie challenged Miguel, who was swaying from side to side.

"Join me, girls—do it like a seat dance," he instructed.

We, of course, swayed with him, and Jackie joined in. I took out my cell and started recording our cupcake shop dance. Everyone played up to the camera. We starting cracking up after a few seconds, feeling extra giddy between the sugar rush and the music.

"Well, back to the studio for us. You all take care! Good seeing you!" Jackie and Miguel gave us big hugs.

"Bye!"

"Hi!" Eliza's mom was at our table just as quickly as the instructors stepped away. "I hate to cut the party short, but we need to be leaving now too."

Eliza and I rose out of our seats slowly, as if trying to stall. We stood facing each other, at a loss for words. Until Eliza cleared her throat and spoke.

"We won't do long good-byes. Just make sure we stay in touch more often than before."

"Weekly video chats?" My voice cracked.

"Weekly," she agreed.

"Perfect," I said.

We reached out and clung to each other.

"See ya," Eliza said as she pulled back.

"See ya."

I stood there watching Eliza wave back one last time before she left the shop with her mom.

It wasn't a great feeling, but I was not carrying it on my own. Lily put an arm around my shoulder, followed by Riley and Trina, and yes, even Megan.

"Let's go home," I told them.

"'m so glad to be home," Megan said, "where it's warm, and I don't have to wear a puffy coat, and there aren't a billion people blocking my way on the sidewalk, and I don't have to ride in an underground hole where rats are."

We all looked at her.

"You didn't like New York?" Riley looked at her. "Does that mean we're not going to be roommates in a penthouse overlooking Central Park?"

"Let's just say I'm glad I got picked for Memphis," Megan said. "No subways."

It did feel good to be back in Florida—and I was not going to complain about the sunshine warming me up. I did like pom-pom hats, though. Maybe I could make them a thing down here. I felt like I had the best of both worlds—summer in New York City and then Florida the rest of the time.

Life was good!

"That's weird," Lily said, looking out the window of the passenger van that shuttled us from the airport. We had just pulled up to the palm-tree-lined plaza where Sugar Plums, Lily's parents' fro-yo shop, and DanceStarz Academy were located.

"Weren't our parents supposed to be picking us up out front of the dance studio?" asked Lily.

"Oh, yeah. Where is everyone?" I asked, concerned at how deserted the parking lot was.

"Was this weekend daylight savings or something?" Trina asked. "I never get that right."

"No," Megan said.

"Maybe when we changed time zones from east to west, it messed up their hours?" Trina suggested.

"Trina, we didn't change time zones." Megan shook her head. "Mom! Where are the other parents? I don't want all these people coming home with us. I'm tired of them."

"Hey!" Riley swatted her.

"It is weird," I said. I fired off texts to my parents. This wasn't like my mom to not be somewhere at the assigned time.

"Did they forget?" Lily asked the unthinkable question everyone was afraid to utter.

"Let's just go inside and I'll start making calls," said Vanessa.

"Don't worry, girls," said Riley's mom. "We'll get to the bottom of this."

We followed Vanessa inside the dark studio. What an anticlimactic return to Florida. The air was heavier, not only because of the humidity, but now because of the swirling emotions weighing us down. Vanessa reached behind the front desk and switched on the lights, and . . .

"SURPRISE!"

We all nearly jumped out of our skin. Well, all of us except Vanessa and the moms, who were clearly in on this. CONGRATULATIONS, DANCESTARZ SQUAD! read a banner overhead with balloons dangling from it.

All of our families were here! Mom, Dad, and Hailey rushed at me, congratulating and hugging me at the same time. Congratu-hugging? I closed my eyes and enjoyed the feeling of their loving, welcoming arms around me. And the feeling of . . . wet slobber?

"Hi, Mo!" I squealed and leaned down to pick up my pup.

Then I reached into my backpack and pulled out presents. Bagels for Mom and Dad. And a stuffed animal wearing an *I heart NY* T-shirt for Hailey.

"It's a Timothy the squirrel!" Hailey squealed, hugging him hard.

I looked around and exchanged glances with Lily, Trina, Megan, and Riley. They looked just as happy as I felt.

"Are you missing New York already?" my dad asked.

"You know what?" I said. "It's good to be home."

This book is about TEAMWORK, so first I want to thank the team who helped bring this book to life:

• The WME|IMG team: Sharon Jackson, Mel Berger, Jenni Levine, Erin O'Brien, Joe Izzi, Matilda Forbes Watson, Josh Otten, Lisa DiRuocco, and everyone at WME|IMG for your support and encouragement.

• The Aladdin team: Starting with Alyson Heller, the driving force behind this book—thank you so much! And to Mara Anastas, Laura DiSiena, Jodie Hockensmith, Nicole Russo, and everyone at Simon and Schuster Children's/Aladdin for your hard work and dedication.

• Rachel Rothman, who has believed in me from the very beginning and was invaluable making this book so awesome!

• Katie Greenthal, Marisa Martins, and everyone at the Lede Company for being such awesome publicists and helping bring my voice out to the world.

• Scott Whitehead and everyone at McKuin, Frankel, Whitehead for all of your wise legal advice.

And:

• Julia DeVillers!! You gave Harper (and the rest of the DanceStarz) an amazing voice and it has been so fun to see these characters come to life. A million thank yous for being such a smart, savvy, and fun partner on this project!

This book is about DANCE, so of course I want to thank all of my friends who have supported me every dance step of the way:

• Sia, who shows me how to be the person I want to be

• All of my dance teachers, who have taught me to be the best I can be

• All of the dancers who have ever shared the dance floor and stage with me. You've motivated and inspired me!

This book is about FAMILY, and you know I love my family so much!

• Kenzie!! My creative and talented sister. You're my best friend and I love you!!

• Gregga, who has always been there for me, supported me and made sure I have whatever I need with patience and positivity—and no complaints!

• Jane, Lilia, and Jack Buckingham, who make LA feel like my home.

• Michelle Young, for all the sleepovers, loud music in the car, and the laughter that never ends.

And:

Mom!! don't know how I got so lucky to have you as my mom. Thank you for everything.

This book is about FOLLOWING YOUR DREAMS. To anyone who has ever watched me, come out to meet me, bought my books and cheered me on as I pursue my passions and follow my dreams in dance, acting, fashion design, makeup, the arts—and just living my life . . .

I want you to know I'm cheering you on, too. I love what I do so much, so thank you for sharing the journey with me. I love you!

Maddie

Don't miss where it all began:

THE AUDITION

NEW YORK TIMES BESTSELLING AUTHOR
MADDIE ZIEGLER

THE AUDITION

I'm standing just offstage, waiting for my big moment. I know my mom and dance teacher are in the audience, holding their breath in anticipation. This will be the most challenging dance I've ever performed—not only that but the most challenging dance anyone at DanceStarz Academy has ever performed. There's a lot of pressure on me.

My costume is amazing—beautifully detailed with thousands of sparkling rhinestones—my makeup is flawless, and my headpiece is sewn in tightly but not so tightly it will give me a screaming headache later.

"You can do it, Harper! Love you, Harper!" My new teammates are encouraging, but I know they're questioning how

this will go. This routine is nearly impossible! How could any twelve-year-old ever possibly pull this off? My adrenaline is racing.

The announcer says:

"Please welcome to the stage: Harper McCoy, performing a solo."

I walk onto the stage, my toes pointed, my head held high. I get into my opening pose and the music begins. Five . . . six . . . seven . . . eight!

And I dance! I'm in the zone as I leap and turn and flip and practically fly. The crowd is gasping. I'm nailing it! And I go into my grand finale: my new signature turn series. I do an insane number of tuck jumps and pirouettes. Twirling, twirling, twirling . . .

The crowd is going wild! The audience is chanting: "Harper! Harper!" My mother's voice in particular stands out from the crowd.

"Harper! Harper!" Mom was whispering loudly. "Stop twirling!"

What? Stop twirling?

I opened my eyes and snapped out of my daydream.

"You're twirling your hair," Mom said quietly.

Oops. I was spacing out. I let go of the piece of hair I was twisting from my ponytail. I wasn't onstage at a competition, amazing the audience. I wasn't even on a competition team—yet. I was sitting in a new chair, in a new dance studio, waiting to audition for a totally new competition team.

"Oh, no!" My eight-year-old sister, Hailey, dramatically fake-gasped and pointed at me from the couch across from me. "It's the apocalypse! Harper has . . . *wispies*!"

My hand flew to the top of my head to smooth any wispies that might have escaped my tight ponytail. I wanted this audition to go perfectly, and that included the details that could distract the judges, like flyaway hair.

"I'm just kidding!" Hailey laughed. "Please. Like Harper didn't use half a can of hairspray this morning."

"Hailey, now isn't a good time for teasing. Your sister is nervous."

"Harper, are you nervous?" Hailey asked.

Um . . . YES?!!

I was about to audition for a new dance studio. I'd be placed in classes (what if I choked and they stuck me in beginner classes with teeny five-year-olds in tutus?) and I'd find out if I could be on a competition team. So, basically my entire life.

Okay, maybe that sounded overly dramatic. But dancing was my life. The dance studio had been my second home since

I was two years old. My mom always said that when I was really little, I would dress up like a fairy princess or a butterfly and jump and twirl around and break things, so she signed me up for a little-kid ballet class to get rid of all that energy. I'd been at that studio ever since.

I took every class they offered: ballet, jazz, tap, lyrical, contemporary. I loved lyrical and contemporary the most, felt confident with my technique in ballet classes, and did tumbling and hip-hop for fun and to help with my routines.

I joined the precompetitive team when I was six and then made the junior competition team. Last year, I started getting solos—and winning with them. My BFFs were on the team with me, and we practiced together almost every day after school.

Don't get me wrong—I liked doing other things besides dancing: drawing, painting, baking brownies, hanging out with my friends, and watching funny YouTube videos (and videos of dancers like Travis Wall and Maddie Ziegler). But the dance floor was my happy place.

A few weeks ago, Dad got a new job in Florida and we had to move pretty quickly.

I cried for a week when Mom and Dad told me; Hailey cried for a week too; even my Mom cried when we packed up our stuff. I definitely didn't want to leave. Eventually, Hailey and Mom said they were up for the adventure of it, but me? I didn't want to say good-bye to my friends and my old life. I didn't want to say good-bye to my old dance studio.

Or hello to a new studio. And new friends.

At least, I *hoped* I'd have a new dance studio. There was a chance they wouldn't even take me on a competition team. When I told my dance teacher back in Connecticut I was moving, she told me that dance was a huge part of Florida culture. That sounded great! Then she told me that Florida had a highly competitive dance community. *HIGHLY* competitive. Eep.

So yeah. I was nervous about this audition at DanceStarz.

"Harper, don't put too much pressure on yourself," Mom said. "If this studio isn't a fit, we can try another one. I just thought since DanceStarz is a newer studio that has only been open a few years, it might be easier for you to acclimate. Be a big fish in a smaller pond."

"Harperfish." Hailey sucked in her cheeks to make a fish face at me. She cracked herself up.

"Also," Mom continued, "DanceStarz is the most convenient to our new house. There's only a few weeks left of summer break, and once school starts, I want to find a job and it would be hard to drive you far. Plus, the other studios have already had competition team tryouts. We're lucky Dance-Starz is letting newcomers audition. Well, worst-case scenario, you could wait until next year. . . ."

"Not helpful, Mom." I raised an eyebrow at her.

"Oh, I'm babbling, aren't I?" My mom smiled at me. "I'm sorry. I just want what's best for you."

I knew my mom got nervous for me too. I did appreciate my mom. Not only did she drive me to the studio practically every day, she had to do things like hot-glue thousands of rhinestones on competition costumes at the last minute and sew my hair into bizarre headpieces with feathers or things while I yelped in pain.

"Mom!" Hailey waved to get my mom's attention. "I need to get something from the car."

"Now?" Mom sighed, then turned to me. "Are you okay alone for a minute?"

"Yes!" Remember how I said I appreciate my dance mom? I also appreciate having her leave—so I can get into my head and into the dance zone, I mean.

I looked around the reception area as I waited. There was a huge DanceStarz logo above the main desk. DanceStarz colors were pink, white, and gold, which I had to admit looked pretty cool. DanceStarz was much brighter than my old studio, with white walls and huge floor-to-ceiling windows. (It was particularly strange to look out the window and see palm trees.)

"Harper!" The woman working the front desk called my name. "Vanessa will see you in fifteen minutes. You may get ready and stretch in Studio C. It's the first door on the left down the corridor."

Here we go.

ive, six, seven, eight.

I counted off as if I were about to start a dance routine while I walked toward the room where my fate would be determined. I passed a vending machine and water fountain as I made my way down the hallway. It was bright too, with the Florida sun streaming in through the windows. I passed Studio A, a huge studio lined with more windows, and Studio B, a smaller one. Nobody was in either of them.

And I reached Studio C.

As I walked in, the scent of the dance studio hit me—a scent that any dancer in the world would recognize: sweaty feet. It smelled like home. Stinky, but like home.

This was smaller than the other two rooms I'd seen. Nobody was in here, either. I slipped out of my white tank and shorts so that I was wearing a black leotard, my most comfortable one, with the crisscross straps in the back.

I could see my reflection in the three mirrored walls of the studio. Oh. Hailey was right. I did have the dreaded wispies. I decided to put my hair up in a dance bun. No wispies, and it would give me something to do to take my mind off my audition. I was an expert at dance buns. I'd done them so many times, I could do it with my eyes closed.

I unzipped my dance duffel. Inside, I had packed all the dance necessities:

Bobby pins
Hairspray
Hair elastics
Extra leotard (black with cami straps)
Tights—pink, in case I had to do ballet
Hairbrush
Bandages
Tape for my feet
Toe pads for my pointe shoes
Water bottle

Packet of trail mix

Towel, because you get sweaty when you dance hard

Deodorant, because see above

Stretch band

And, of course, I'd had to pack a lot of shoes: my ballet shoes, pointe shoes, jazz and tap shoes. Even though I was going to do a contemporary routine for my audition, I wanted to be extra prepared.

I had also brought a few other things:

Vanilla-scented spray (Remember the stinky studio? A quick spritz of this and at least *I* smelled better).

Fuzzy socks with grippers to keep my feet warm. Black-and-white-striped with a zebra face on the toes. I know, super cute!

Pins stuck on the outside of the bag that my dance team friends had given me as going-away presents to remember them forever and always! Except—sorry, guys—right now I had to forget about them. I had to focus on my future. Not just focus—*hyper*focus, and dance my heart out.

I grabbed some hairpins and my hairspray from the bag and went to the mirror to put my long, medium-brown hair up into a bun. I redid my ponytail (no wispies!) and twisted it into a tight "rope." I wrapped the "rope" around the hair elastic, flattening it out a little and securing it with hairpins—lots of hairpins. Then I tucked the end under tightly and pinned it some more. I finished with a heavy dose of hairspray to freeze it into place.

Bun was done.

I unzipped the shoe compartment, stuck in my flip-flops, and pulled out my half-soles. These were shoes that covered the top half of my feet and had a strap across them but were open at the heel. These were the best shoes for a variety of dance styles, like contemporary or lyrical, so I wouldn't slip on the floor. I sat down on the rubbery marley floor and pulled on a shoe. I winced as I hit a blister, but pulled the shoe on all the way. Blisters came with the territory. So did sore muscles, scabs, and bruises. Us dancers are tough.

I was ready to stretch. As any teacher will tell you a million times, because it's true, stretching warms up muscles, increases flexibility, and helps prevent injuries. I stood up and began with neck rolls. I could see myself in the mirror as I rolled my head to the left and then to the right. Then I did some shoulder rolls.

Just as I started side stretches, the door opened.

And a giant trophy walked in—with my little sister's legs and slightly lighter-than-mine brown pigtails sticking out from behind it. *Oh my gosh. Hailey.* That trophy was almost as big as she was.

"Weeeeeee are the champions, my friend!" the trophy sang. "And we'll keep on fighting—"

"Hailey, what are you doing with my trophy?" I asked her. "And what are you doing in here?!"

"You were nervous, so I'm reminding you who you are. You're a champion dancer!" Hailey triumphantly placed the trophy on the floor in front of me. "Like it says on the plaque. *Top Junior Solo of the World.*"

"Not exactly the world." I had to grin. "At nationals."

"Oh. Actually, I never really read the plaque. Well, nationals is still pretty good, I guess," Hailey reassured me.

Nationals was more than pretty good. It was amazing! It was held in New Jersey, so close to New York City you could see skyscrapers through the windows of the convention center. I had danced a lyrical solo. I'd loved my intricate choreography, the beautiful music, and my shimmery costume. After I'd danced, I'd watched the crowd jump up from their seats and cheer. Including my mom and sister. My sister might be annoying, but she really was my biggest cheerleader.

"Thanks, Hailey. Seriously," I said. "But now, please hide the trophy, and you need to go!"

"Hide it?" Hailey asked. "But I was going to show your teacher. When she comes in, I'll announce you like: *Drumroll, please ... introducing the top junior soloist of the nation: Harper!"*

Hailey proceeded to fangirl around me, jumping around and squealing and acting like she was going to faint.

"Hailey, you're amazing, but that's enough!" I said. Someone might come in the room and see this! What if that someone was Miss Vanessa? Or other people auditioning? I didn't want anyone to think I brought my trophy—and my own crazed superfan—with me! *Uh, Mom? A little help here?* Where was that dance mom now that I needed her?

"I can't believe I'm in the same room as Harper!" Hailey was enjoying this way too much. "I luuuuurve you!"

I did what I had to do to get Hailey out of here. For some reason, Hailey hated hugs. So I grabbed her and squeezed her super tight into a bear hug.

"I luuuurve you too," I said.

"Ack! You're squashing me! Let me go!"

"Only if you take that trophy back to the car," I said.

The door opened and I gasped. Fortunately, it was just my mother.

"Hailey, where did you go? Are you two wrestling? And can you tell me why you wanted to bring Harper's trophy in here?" my mom asked. "You know what, I don't even want to know anymore."

"Mom, we gotta go back to the car! Quick!" Hailey said. I loosened my grip, and Hailey picked up the trophy and raced out the door.

So sweet. But so potentially embarrassing.

I sat down on the floor and did some leg stretches. The door opened again, and this time a girl came in. She had her black hair in a bun at the nape of her neck and was wearing a black halter-style leotard. She was looking at her phone and didn't see me.

"11:11," she said to herself.

"Make a wish!" I blurted out. I would have felt stupid about eavesdropping, except the girl said, "Make a wish!" exactly the same time I did. We both laughed.

"Close your eyes," the girl said.

I closed my eyes. Of course my wish was that my audition would go well and I'd make the competition team. When I opened my eyes, the girl was opening hers, too.

"Hope our wishes come true," I said.

"Me too," the girl said. "Sorry to barge in on you, by the way. They told me to come and cool down from my audition. Oh, just so you know? The audition's not too bad."

I let out a big sigh of relief.

The door opened again.

"Harper, Vanessa is ready for you."